DEADLIER THAN NVA SNIPERS WERE HIS SO-CALLED ALLIES—SECRET ARVN ASSASSINS

His Montagnard bodyguards chased a crowd of camp Vietnamese from Bendell's jeep. But nobody saw the hands that opened the gas tank and slipped something inside.

Heading down the runway at forty-five miles per hour, he slowed quickly to accommodate the dip at the black-top's end. It was then that the explosion occurred. Bendell dived to his left through a wall of flame . . .

Legs shaking, the lanky officer sat down and watched his now blackened vehicle, totally engulfed in flame as it sent tongues of fire and black smoke shooting up into the hot sky . . .

CROSSBOW

DON BENDELL

BERKLEY BOOKS, NEW YORK

CROSSBOW

A Berkley Book/published by arrangement with
the author

PRINTING HISTORY
Berkley edition/July 1990

ISBN: 0-425-12173-9

A BERKLEY BOOK® TM 757,375
Berkley Books are published by The Berkley Publishing Group,
200 Madison Avenue, New York, New York 10016.
The name ''BERKLEY'' and the ''B'' logo
are trademarks belonging to Berkley Publishing Corporation.

PRINTED IN THE UNITED STATES OF AMERICA

10 9 8 7 6 5 4 3 2 1

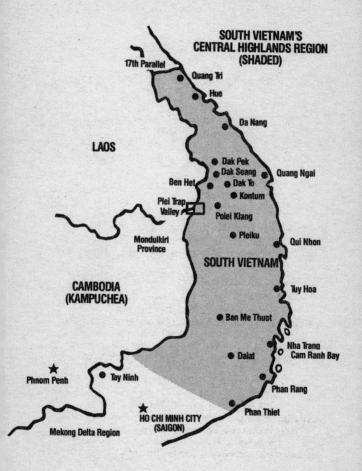

SOUTH VIETNAM'S
CENTRAL HIGHLANDS REGION
(SHADED)

17th Parallel

Quang Tri

Hue

Da Nang

LAOS

Dak Pek
Dak Seang
Ben Het
Dak To
Plei Trap
Valley
Kontum
Polei Kiang
Mondulkiri
Province
Pleiku

Quang Ngai

Qui Nhon

SOUTH VIETNAM

Tuy Hoa

CAMBODIA
(KAMPUCHEA)

Ban Me Thuot

Nha Trang
Cam Ranh Bay

Dalat

Phnom Penh

Tay Ninh

Phan Rang

HO CHI MINH CITY
(SAIGON)

Phan Thiet

Mekong Delta Region

WHAT YOU ARE ABOUT TO READ IS A TRUE STORY.
NO NAMES HAVE BEEN CHANGED, BUT WE PRAY
THAT MANY HEARTS WILL BE.

THIS BOOK IS DEDICATED TO THE MEN AND WOMEN OF THE
U.S. ARMY SPECIAL FORCES AND IN MEMORY OF ALL AMERI-
CAN SOLDIERS WHO LIVED, LOVED, FOUGHT, AND DIED WITH
AND FOR THE MONTAGNARD (DEGA) TRIBESPEOPLE OF THE
CENTRAL HIGHLANDS REGION OF SOUTH VIETNAM, LAOS, AND
KAMPUCHEA (CAMBODIA).

THE STRONGEST FEAR

by
Don Bendell

The jungle loomed in front of me
Across a dark green sea.
"If we can cross this open space,
Then we will be home free."

Halfway across we made it then.
"We won't get killed today!"
A hollow thud, another one;
Two mortars on the way!

"Hey, Sergeant, tell those men, 'Get down'
Unless they want to die!"
Ka-boom . . . it missed, ka-boom . . . it too,
"Thank God . . . Get up . . . Oh my!"

Five minutes more . . . ka-boom, ka-boom . . .
The dirt flew in my face.
None dead . . . "Get up!"
Start moving out!
Tell point speed up the pace!"

Five minutes more . . . ka-boom! ka-boom!
The rounds came for an hour,
But then they stopped. "Be ready, men!
We'll show them firepower!"

The silence of the jungle roared.
My heart throbbed in my chest.
"Oh, please, dear Lord, don't let me die;
Please help me pass this test?"

I knew I'd die. I felt a fear,
A fear I'd never known.
I wouldn't cry or shed a tear.
In six months I'd go home.

The fight began, and then I heard,
"You die, American!"
To hell with fear! To hell with death!
To hell with all of them!"

The noise was like a thousand drums,
A symphony of hate.
"Assault on line! And shoot to kill!
Don't miss! We'll lose! Don't wait!"

The bullets cracked. The screams were loud.
My men were making kills.
We fought for strength; "In courage, men,
Now damn, let's take that hill!"

Some hours passed, we took the hill
And cut a landing zone.
A chopper came. The wounded left.
The dead were taken home.

And then it came; I lit a smoke . . .
My knees began to shake,
And then my arms, and then my head,
And all my muscles ached.

My bladder ached; tears filled my eyes;
My bumps and cuts were sore;
A total fear had raped my mind . . .
But why did I want more?

FOREWORD

Montagnard is a French word meaning "mountain people." The Dega, or Montagnards, are a nomadic tribespeople who inhabit the jungle-covered mountains primarily in South Vietnam's Central Highlands but are also found in the mountainous interiors of Laos and Kampuchea (Cambodia). There are thirty-two distinct tribes of Montagnards, each with its own language and customs. A totally different race from the Vietnamese, most tribes are Mongoloid in appearance, having descended from the Mon-Khmer ethnic groups. A few tribes, however, such as the Rhade and Jarai, are somewhat taller with a slightly different look, having descended from the Indo-Polynesian racial groups. All are much more stocky and brown-skinned than the Vietnamese. A very proud, happy, spiritual, warlike, but family-oriented society, they use the "slash-and-burn" method for growing rice. In essence, they will cut and burn away a large section of jungle, then grow and harvest rice until the area is overworked after several years. Then they move the village to a new location.

In most of the tribes the women wear only a black silk wraparound skirt and are bare-breasted. The men usually wear only a black loincloth. Both men and women wear many brass bracelets, necklaces, and earrings. Some tribes also make and wear simple beaded necklaces. While some tribes find gold-capped teeth to be fashionable, still other tribes literally file their teeth into fangs. A male-dominated society, the men do the hunting, fighting, fishing, and toolmaking, while the women are responsible for cooking, weaving, cutting firewood, sewing, basket weaving, growing and harvesting rice, and, of course, bearing children. The latter, however, is done quite differently from most modern-day birthing techniques. Around the eighth month of pregnancy the husband prepares a secret birthing hut in the jungle. At the onset of labor, the expectant mother travels to the hut, delivers her child alone, and returns to her work while the newborn infant nurses, held by a scarf worn around her neck.

Some Montagnard villages are a series of bamboo-interwoven longhouses on stilts set in neat rows, while other villages have longhouses on stilts with thatched roofs and underground bunkers. Many villages are surrounded by a seven-foot wooden wall, on the outside of which are placed millions of punji stakes pointing outward in all directions to ward off would-be attackers. Punji stakes are bamboo sticks sharpened to a razor-sharp point.

Besides rice and vegetables, villagers eat bats, rats, monkeys, snakes, bugs, fish, and other jungle creatures. Many Dega men enjoy drinking rice wine.

A severe racial problem has existed between the Dega and the Vietnamese for years. In a declaration issued on May 27, 1946, the government of France recognized the Dega's autonomy, as well as recognizing the Central Highlands as the Montagnards' own country, which the French called Pays du Montagnard du Hauts-Plateaux du Indochinois. The Vietnamese dictator Ngo Dinh Diem had different ideas, however, and started moving Vietnamese into the Central Highlands, instituting a policy of discrimination and outright slaughter of the Dega that continues to this day. The Dega still have no schools, no right to vote, no representation in government. Out of this suppression sprang a secret Montagnard movement called FULRO, which is an acronym originally for Front Unifié des Luttes des Race-Oprimees but which is now called Front United for the Liberation of the Racially Oppressed. Crossing all tribal boundaries, FULRO recruited members from all thirty-two tribes, with the goal of regaining the Central Highlands and the Dega's own autonomy. In mid-1964, FULRO orchestrated a bloody coup attempt throughout the Central Highlands. The very pro-American Montagnards struck at Special Forces A-camps in a coordinated attack. American Green Berets were locked up and guarded in their team houses, while Vietnamese in the camps were hung from flagpoles and dropped into latrine seats and then machine-gunned. Because of their happy nature, simple honesty, extreme courage, and unflagging loyalty to the Americans, many Dega endeared themselves to the Green Berets who lived with them and who still cry over the plight of this proud race. This is the true story of the man who is the president of the FULRO, and his best friend and Senior Adviser, a former Green Beret officer who lived with the Jeh tribe in 1968 and early 1969, and who became obsessed with their plight.

... 1 ...

A DAY IN THE LIFE OF ...

Bark! Bark! Bark! The noise broke the stillness of the jungle morning. Bark! Bark! Bark! Beautiful flaming orange strands of hair hung from the sinewy arms of an orangutan high in the dark green jungle canopy, his eyes lazily sweeping the dark and muddy floor below. Bark! Bark! His eyes caught a slight movement and the noisemaker was identified: A barking deer two feet in height was bellowing a bold challenge to would-be intruders. The ape related; the little noisemaker was not a threat. The mighty orange ape could see a Sedang Montagnard village on a partially bare hilltop seven hundred yards down the emerald ridge line. His eyes detected movement but couldn't make out what it was. "No danger" was his instinct. "Too far away."

Shiny beads of sweat flew left and right from tanned young breasts. The two Montagnard sisters were too engaged in early-morning gossip to pay attention to the already mounting heat and humidity from the crucifying Vietnamese climate.

Chim, the older sister, who was sixteen, kept swatting at pesky flies as she told the latest exploits of her oldest child. Sal, the fifteen-year-old, just giggled at each story. She balanced a woven bamboo basket on top of her head,

4

raven-colored hair flowing all the way down over her very shapely buttocks. Her even, white teeth and innocence gave her a quiet beauty. While giggling at her older sister's stories, she marveled at Chim and her strength at being able to carry the 250-pound load of firewood on her back and talk easily and effortlessly about her children. She envied Chim's beauty and maturity. The Dega grew up fast, especially during continual days of war, and Chim could as easily have been forty as sixteen. Sweat flowed freely on the women's well-shaped bodies as they walked through the village, by giggling children and laughing faces at family cook fires. In the background, beyond the ominous village wall, mountains towered, each covered with a steaming hot emerald-green carpet. Wood smoke, body odor, and the smells of cooking monkey and bamboo shoots hung strong in the humid air . . . the smells of home. A worried look appeared on Chim's pretty face as the two reached her cook fire and put down their respective loads.

Sal spoke. "What is wrong, Sister?"

"Oh, nothing, Sal. I just worry about Ek. He left yesterday to hunt and has not returned. His cousin was eaten by a tiger just last week. The Vietcong are always patrolling in the jungle—"

Laughing, Sal interrupted. "I think, big sister, that you worry too much. Look."

Chim turned her head and breathed a sigh of relief as she saw a smiling, well-muscled man approach, a small bamboo crossbow and arrows in one hand and three very large dead jungle rats in the other. He proudly held them up to show his wife, then dropped them by the fire.

Ek spoke. "Hello, Sal . . . hello, beautiful wife. Did you miss me?"

She smiled and replied, "You big, silly monkey. Did I miss you? Does the krait slither through the grass? You hunted well, Ek. Today we eat good. You must eat with us, little sister, please?"

Giggling again, Sal looked down at her shapely calves. "No, I can fix my own food, thank you."

"Nonsense," Chim replied. "Your husband hunts too far in the jungle. You eat with us."

Sal, still giggling, retorted, "Okay, okay, thank you."

The two women started preparing the rats to eat as Ek pulled a machete-sized knife from a bamboo sheath and started sharpening it with a whetstone. The blade, larger than a bowie knife, was made from the shrapnel from a five-hundred-pound bomb and had little brass inlays in the back of the blade. Sedang (Ek's tribe) symbols were engraved into the massive blade. The handle was made of highly polished water-buffalo horn. The beautiful knife was a work of craftsmanship and had been a gift to Ek from the village blacksmith, his father. Lighting a pipe, he looked over at his pretty wife and two of his giggling children playing just beyond the fire. He smiled in love and contentment.

Thwack! Ek jumped quickly to his feet and turned around. A grin spread across his face as he looked at the impish grin on the face of his four-year-old son, who had just splattered him with a mud ball. The boy giggled and ran as his father ran after him, growling like a tiger.

Giggling, the boy ran from his growling father. "Dei Ba! Dei Ba! (No, Dad!)" he yelled, laughing so hard that the words were barely discernible.

The mood was much more somber, the setting much stiffer, in a spit-polished U.S. Army briefing room in Saigon. Two MPs stood at parade rest on either side of the door. Their faces were expressionless, a real accomplishment by the one on the left, as he really wanted to cry behind his stone mask. He had a painful dose of the clap, acquired from a fifteen-year-old "virgin" who finally had decided to sell herself to feed her poor, ailing mamasan.

The spit-polished floor tile looked as if it were covered with a three-foot-thick layer of glass, the effect of which was achieved by liberal doses of Butcher's Red Wax and elbow grease, both applied with clean, new Birdseye Diapers. A platoon of news reporters and several squads of photographers stood and sat around the room, recorders, cameras, and pencils poised and ready to strike. Unwitting pawns in the War of News Headlines, they stood ready to be fed a new barrage of inflated body counts and understated enemy troop strength reports. Seated behind the giant mahogany conference table were an American and a Vietnamese general, both in class-A uniforms. They gave each other nervous here-we-go-again nods, then, trying hard to hide themselves behind the two little table microphones, they opened the floor for questions.

A sandy-haired reporter in cut-off Levi's and a heavily sweat-stained safari shirt raised his hand. "General, what about the Montagnard tribespeople in the Central Highlands? Do you really believe they're going to fight for your government? They have no right to vote, no representation, no schools, no equal rights whatsoever."

Interrupting, sweaty palms in the air, the five-foot-tall general of the Army of the Republic of Vietnam (ARVN) leaned into his microphone. Flash bulbs and strobes blazed as he spoke, a phony smile spreading across his face. "Wait, I will be happy to answer you. The Montagnards are quite happy to help us because they know that the communists are evil. Our government in Saigon cares about them very much."

A French journalist spoke up. "*Mon genéral*, why do zey have no schools? Why can zey not vote een zeir own country? What about zeir rights? You have not answered zeese questions."

Hands up again, the commander said, "Well, you see, these people are primitive. They really have no need for schools. They wouldn't know how to vote." Laughing nervously he continued. "How could they vote? They can't even read or write."

The Parisian went on. "*Genéral*, let's get very honest,

s'il vous plaît. For years your police and military have gone eento Montagnard villages. Zey zen peeck out men who are strong or intelligent or both, and zen accuse zem either of consorting weeth your enemies or being involved in zee FULRO movement, and zey are executed. Why does your government fear zee Montagnard so? Why are you so frightened by zee FULRO? Do you worry zat zey will be successful in overtrowing Saigon and taking back zee Central Highlands?''

By this time the general was bubbling with fury, but the reporter added, ''Tell me, *Général*. Could your people just simply treat zee Montagnards like human beings? Would zat not be much simpler?''

Furiously slamming both fists on the table, the general, red-faced, veins bulging on his neck and forehead, jumped to his feet, ''*Choi oi!*'' he raged. ''*Choi duc oi!* Lies! These are lies! We do not do such things! The Central Highlands are part of Vietnam! Those savages shouldn't be in our country. There is no FULRO! Bah!'' Turning to the general, he hissed, ''He, he made me lose face!''

With that the tiny officer, still seething, stormed out of the crowded briefing room, brushing by a photographer on the way, his uniform jacket against the man's lit cigar, singeing the tailored garment. The American general stood up, microphone in hand.

Holding his hand up in a calming gesture, he said, ''Gentlemen, ladies, please. the South Vietnamese are our allies . . . our friends. They want and need our help and support so that their country won't fall into the hands of the communists. Let's not anger them. Please try to understand.''

Chim went into the family's little underground bunker to get a small basket she had been working on and was followed by Ek, who had run out of tobacco. As he bent over her, with a laugh he ran his hand quickly up the inside of her thigh.

"A rat attacks you!" He chuckled.

"And a wife is going to attack you, Ek, if you don't behave," she replied, slapping his arm.

The two exited the bunker and rejoined Sal. Ek sat down, picked up the last bite of rat and ate it. He threw the tail in the fire, wiped his hands on his arms, and stretched. Just then a great hush fell over the village. The two women looked at each other questioningly as Ek quickly picked up his crossbow and arrows.

Walking toward the center of the village, he tried to reassure his concerned wife. "It's probably the American missionary, who has come to tell us more about Jesus."

The one wooden gate in the seven-foot wooden wall opened, and through it walked a platoon of ARVN soldiers, led by a skinny lieutenant carrying a swagger stick and wearing a phony, gold-toothed smile. The soldiers looked around them with condescension. The lieutenant was met at the center of the hilltop hamlet by the village chief, an older man named Roi.

Folding his skinny arms across his ribby chest, the lieutenant said, "I am Thieu-uy Tran, of the Army of the Republic of Vietnam. Are you the chief of this village?"

Roi nodded. "I am chief. I am called Roi." He proudly jabbed a stubby brown thumb into his own chest.

Tran looked about at the gathered listeners. "You Montagnards are the government's children. I have been sent here by the government in Saigon, which loves your people and wishes to protect you."

Roi spoke proudly and firmly. "We are Sedang. We can protect ourselves."

Temper flaring, Tran blurted, "You don't argue with me, *moi*!" Then, quckly calming himself, he continued. "How much rice do you have?"

"Just enough for my people" came the terse reply.

With an air of confidence, even arrogance, Tran moved forward, responding quietly. "Your village will give us one fourth of all your rice, and when my men need food, such as now, you will supply us with pigs and chickens and dogs to eat. The government needs your taxes in order to protect you."

Masking his anger, Roi queried, "Tell me, Thieu-uy, are the Vietcong and North Vietnamese soldiers bad people?"

"Of course," the lieutenant responded angrily. "The communists are butchers. They are demons. Why do you even ask?"

Roi answered calmly, "The VC come into our village and demand our rice and animals. They kill our men. They rape our women. You and your soldiers do the same thing. Tell me, what is the difference between you and the communists? I think it is just the name and the uniform."

Teeth clenched together, Tran pulled out a U.S. Army Colt .45 automatic and said, "Did you say that you have given rice to the Vietcong?"

Roi smiled. "I do not like to walk the same path twice. You heard me. Like we are forced to with you."

Tran lifted and cocked the pistol and grinned, the barrel a scant two inches in front of Roi's forehead. "You have consorted with the enemy!"

He pulled the trigger. The explosion of the gun was joined by the loud screams and wails of several women; bits of brain matter and blood splattered on half a dozen onlookers. Roi's wife ran forward and threw herself across his lifeless body; racking sobs came from her dirty, naked chest.

Smiling wickedly at his men, the wimpy officer rested the gun's barrel against the back of her head and said, "She must also be a Vietcong sympathizer."

The trigger was pulled again.

With a nod from Lieutenant Tran, several soldiers seized five muscular young men and brought them forward to him.

Looking them over, he said, still brandishing the pistol, "You five have also been consorting with the enemy."

A sixteen-year-old warrior spoke out bravely. "You make up these lies to wipe out our people. We would not consort with any Yuan. Why don't you stop lying and just kill us?"

Tran grinned and raised his pistol as a scream rang out, and all heads turned.

"Dei! Dei! Dei bang!" A little gray-haired lady ran forward and fell at the legs of the sixteen-year-old.

Wrapping her wrinkled arms around his calves, she cried and shook her head no.

Tran shot him through the heart. He aimed at the next man, and the thirteen-year-old spit in his face. The wailing was loud and long as flies buzzed around the five new bodies heaped on the hard-packed earth.

Angrily Tran yelled to the villagers, "At the end of each harvest this village will deliver to Province Headquarters one fourth—no, one half—of all your rice!"

Looking around at the crowd's reactions, he spotted Chim and Sal. Another evil grin spread across his face as he motioned for the duo to be seized and brought forward. They were brought forward, kicking and screaming, after Ek had to be knocked down by a vicious butt stroke from a rifle.

For several seconds Tran stared lustfully at the two women, and with a quick movement he tore away both of their skirts, leaving them standing naked in front of them all. He shoved Sal to his platoon sergeant and grabbed Chim by the arm.

He said quietly to the platoon sergeant, "That one is for your men, and this one is for me." Then he yelled to the grim-faced villagers, "My men and I will show you that we love your people."

Chim was quiet as he ran his fingers all over her breasts, but she let out a cry and a whimper as he forced his finger between her vaginal lips. Sweat dripped down his face and he grinned maliciously.

"On your knees, woman," he commanded. "And open that pretty mouth."

~~Neither~~ the whooshing sound nor the slight *thunk* was barely audible as the tiny bamboo arrow embedded itself right between Lieutenant Tran's eyes. They slightly crossed and then rolled back into his head as the now dead officer toppled backward into a nearby cook fire. Tran could not feel the flames that quickly burned the hair from his head. All eyes turned toward Ek as he quickly loaded another arrow onto his crossbow.

The quickly fired arrow caught another ARVN soldier—the one holding Sal—in the heart as Ek quickly unsheathed his knife and charged the remaining soldiers, emitting a bloodcurdling scream. Numerous Vietnamese fired their weapons simultaneously, but Ek, his muscular torso riddled with bullets, would not give up. With his machetelike knife slashing wildly, he cut left and right, killing three more ARVN soldiers and severely wounding another. Blood rushing to the ground from a dozen wounds, his mighty body finally gave up as he crashed to the ground, the hysterical scream of Chim in his ears. A pop-eyed soldier stabbed his lifeless body over and over again with his bayonet while Chim and Sal quickly replaced their skirts.

Grave-faced and determined, armed only with knives and spears, the rest of the village men slowly walked forward toward the ARVN soldiers. The heavily armed Vietnamese soldiers seemed to realize as they looked at the determined Dega faces that this truly would be a fight to the death. Visibly shaken and frightened, they quickly backed to the village gate and funneled out, fleeing into the nearby jungle.

The report that was later filed by the ARVN described a ferocious battle with elements of the 66th NVA Regiment—resulting in heroic deaths for Lieutenant Tran, his men, and numerous NVA soldiers, of course.

Slapping a muddy little hand on his father's unmoving

chest, Ek's small, naked son cried out, "Ba! Ba! Ba!" Sedang for Father! Father! Father!

Unconcerned, the mighty orange orangutan looked away from the commotion down the hill and turned his attention to a pesky flea in his long sorrel hair. He picked it out, bit it, and tossed it away. Then he reached for the hard body of a tick under his left arm as he glanced at panting soldiers running through the thick jungle down below.

... 2 ...

THE GUERRILLA

With mist holding low over the vast swamp, stumps poking through it like eerie sentinels in the night, the scene was reminiscent of a sequence in *King Kong*. A sliver of moonlight, giving a scary cast to numerous shadows on the water's surface, made the setting even more frightening. A long and rickety beaver dam ran along one end of the bog for about one hundred yards. At the far side of the pond the ground suddenly jutted upward, as if trying to escape this eerie environment. The steep hillside, covered with stately pine, oak, and maple, was blanketed with a thick green carpet of dark, wet undergrowth.

On top of the wooded hill a crusty old first sergeant raised a canteen cup to his lips. He wore scars from service in Korea and South Vietnam. The coffee burned his lips, but that was how he liked it, and it was a pleasant diversion from the idiotic rantings of his company commander, an ROTC-graduated captain who paced back and forth in front of the campfire, thoroughly chewing the ass of his officers and NCOs. Top, the First Sergeant, took it with a grain of salt and feigned interest. A survivor for twenty-two years, he knew how to play the game.

Slapping the butt of the .45 on his hip, the captain concluded, "Well, gentlemen, if there are no questions, you're all dismissed. I suggest a good night's sleep. Tomorrow we're gonna kick some commie-gook ass.''

A lone lieutenant, the company executive officer, raised his hand. ''Uh, sir, excuse me.''

Frustrated, the captain put his hands on his hips and sighed. ''Yeah, Lieutenant, what is it?''

''Sir, I just noticed today that the side of our perimeter that faces the swamp is really weak, and I just wondered if it shouldn't be beefed up some? The VC might—''

Interrupting, the now red-faced captain asked, ''Lieutenant, how long ago did you graduate from OC fucking S?''

''Six months, sir.''

''Six months, huh?'' The officer glared. ''Six fucking months and you're going to tell me about tactics. Well, Lieutenant, I got numerous likely enemy avenues of approach and only about two hundred swingin' dicks in this company to cover our asses. With all the water, stumps, tangles, and shit in that bog, the fuckin' commie slopes ain't about to swim or wade, and they ain't got boats, which wouldn't fuckin' make it, anyway. That's why our perimeter is lighter there, and the men put to better use where the enemy is more likely to probe or try an infiltration. That is why I wear railroad tracks on my collar and you're just a fuckup second balloon that's still wet behind the ears. Understand, Lieutenant?''

Ears burning from embarrassment, the young officer turned away. ''Yes, sir.''

Grinning, the captain moved toward his tent. ''Good night, gentlemen.''

Six silent shadows paused at the edge of the pond and gazed at the hillside, muffled voices filtering through the darkened woods near the summit. Bending down, they removed their shoes, which were tied together and hung around their necks. Sweat dripped off their black pajama bottoms and onto their muddy, bare feet as the small patrol all held hands with one other and, feeling with their toes, inched their way across the flimsy beaver dam. Several times branches gave way and tumbled down into the quicksand-filled swamp below. The patrol leader halted, and then each man tried to stop breathing, so as not to cause undue pressure on the structure.

After forty-five minutes they reached solid ground at the end of the fragile, hundred-yard structure. At a silent hand signal from the leader, they dropped to the ground and replaced their shoes. Standing, each automatically checked his weapon and ammunition. With another hand signal, the patrol glided silently upward, swallowed by the wooded darkness.

Two nervous PFCs stared at the overwhelming blackness from their wombish foxhole. They hated being assigned to this listening post, sixty meters out from their company perimeter, connected only by two strands of black Army commo wire. The field telephone, their panic button, was more important to them than their M16s, which they now clutched tightly. Neither knew that a pair of hands were deftly cutting through both strands of wire with a razor-sharp Kabar knife, hands jutting out from two loose black cotton pajama sleeves.

Willy and Billy were from two totally different worlds but were bonded together in a closeness unlike any friendship. They were bonded by fear. Willy, black, had grown up in Harlem hating whites, all whites. Billy had grown up just outside Fayetteville, North Carolina, on a tobacco farm less than ten miles from a large billboard along a major highway that proudly showed a Klansman in white hood and robe on a rearing white horse, bearing the bold statement: WELCOME! YOU ARE ENTERING THE HEART OF KLAN COUNTRY.

Right now both stared into a black void, acting brave for each other. Both knew something was wrong . . . but what?

Billy picked up the handset on the field phone just as three black shadows dropped into the foxhole from above. There were brief sounds of a struggle and moaning, then only the sounds of crickets. The three black shadows eased out of the hole and glided noiselessly up the hill.

Those along the perimeter were less wary, each feeling the false sense of security of greater numbers, each knowing that Willy and Billy would be sitting wide-eyed sixty meters out, straining their senses at every sound and smell.

This laxity was the reason the two playing cards in the bottom of their foxhole were not much of a fight for the shadows that dropped in. The one who had fallen asleep on the lip of his foxhole, his flabby chin resting on the butt of his M16 rifle, proved even easier to silence. And so the black figures noiselessly popped in and out of seven foxholes along the eastern perimeter. They glided toward the company command post.

The man who had silenced the commo wire as easily wrote down the radio frequency in a small notebook from the AN-PRC-25 radio that lightly crackled by the unattended campfire.

Another raised the blackened pot and poured cups of steaming coffee for several of his pajama-clad comrades. Another opened the flap of the captain's tent and, with a hiss and pop, pulled the pin on two smoke grenades, tossing them in. He brought a battered Vietcong bugle to his lips and blew triumphantly.

Simultaneously his comrades dropped their coffee cups, tossed the Americans' operations maps and various other maps into the fire, and opened up with their weapons in all directions. With yells and whoops they took off down the ridge line, apparently planning to shoot an exit for themselves through the company perimeter.

A cry rang out from one of the black-clothed warriors: "You die, you Yankee motherfuckers! You die!"

In the meantime Americans all over the perimeter started shooting at the Vietcong, shadows, trees, and each other.

A great cry rang up amid gunfire, explosions, pops, and screams as the enemy patrol burst through the southeastern end of the perimeter.

Swallowed up by the darkness, they silently weaved in and out among the trees, leaving behind them gunfire, shouts, and curses.

Chuckling at the disruption of the American company still firing wildly from the distant hilltop, the VC patrol emerged on a hard-packed dirt road. Knowing pursuit was imminent, they immediately started hiding under stones in the roads pyrotechinic booby traps that inevitably would get kicked out of the way. Two strung a black string across the road, the end of which was connected to an explosive booby trap wired five feet up in a sapling along the road-side.

Coughing and hacking, the now enraged captain tried to lace up his jungle boots as he barked orders, trying to restore order. Just then his lieutenant ran by and stopped, a self-satisfied grin fighting to spread across his face. Veins bulged out the embarrassed and furious company commander's neck and face.

"Get the fuck outa here smart-ass!" he screamed. "Top! Top!"

"Over here, sir," the beefy first sergeant yelled.

"Top," the captain growled. "Leave the weapons platoon here in reserve and saddle up the rest of the company! We're gonna run those commie gook bastards down!"

Having been around enough to know the futility of arguing the stupidity and danger of giving pursuit in the darkness, Top simply responded, "Yes, sir!"

Within ten minutes the company was armed, assembled, and sweeping down the ridge line in pursuit of the enemy patrol.

A half hour later, on the dirt road, the VC patrol leader held up his hand, and the others halted, alert to danger from any direction. Behind them, several of their booby traps went off, followed by rifle and machine-gun fire.

Their leader grinned in the darkness when he smelled the rainstorm forming. It would hide their tracks and make the "weak American infantrymen" even more miserable.

On his signal, the patrol slowly and cautiously eased forward, toward the American-looking white frame house that now loomed before them. Complete with a yard, picket fence, and garage, the house looked so American and so out of place in this setting. Some windows showed light, and muffled sounds came from the back part of the house. The silent patrol glided toward it.

As the sounds became louder and the lights brighter, the squad moved more slowly and quietly. At the back of the house, the leader crept up to the porch door and looked in.

On the floor, a boy of about nine years old was seated at the feet of what apparently was his white-haired grandfather, who sat in a recliner. Across the room, his grandmother hummed while sewing patches on a Cub Scout uniform. All three laughed at a joke made by Johnny Carson on the color TV. The patrol leader knocked on the door and saw the grandmother and grandfather jump up, startled, and move to the door, turning on the porch light.

Opening the door, they looked out at the muddy and disheveled patrol. All six were Americans clad in black pajamas, tennis shoes, and wearing red-flashed green berets on their heads. The leader's beret sported a shiny, gold second lieutenant's bar. The biggest man carried an M-60 machine gun and had several crossed belts of ammo across his chest. The rest carried M16 rifles. They all had knives, ammo belts with harnesses, various smoke grenades, artillery simulators, and other explosive training devices.

The leader, the second lieutenant, wore a battered Vietcong bugle around his neck, he was tall with short brown hair and had piercing hazel eyes with a little bit of a twinkle in them.

Removing his beret, he spoke softly. "Excuse me, ma'am. Sorry to disturb you folks . . . and . . . uh . . .

scare you with our appearance. I'm Lieutenant Don Bendell with Company C of the Seventh Special Forces Group, out of Fort Bragg, North Carolina, and—''

At this, the excited young boy interrupted. ''Oh, wow, Grandpa! Green Berets!''

Grinning, Bendell continued, ''Anyway, we've been taking part in a field training exercise here in Virginia against the Third Infantry Regiment, the Old Guard from Washington, D.C. Unfortunately, to help train them, we have to be the bad guys . . . the Vietcong.''

The woman threw her hands up, ''Oh, my, how exciting!''

''I'm really sorry to bother you folks so late, but my men have been working very hard tonight, and we have about two hundred very angry people chasing us. Could my men possibly fill their canteens from your garden hose?''

At this, the old man stepped forward, hitching up his pants. ''Hell, no!'' he growled. ''You're Green Berets! It's starting to rain . . . get inside. We'll hide ya and feed ya. How 'bout some hot coffee?''

The woman interjected, ''Oh, I just made a batch of chocolate-chip cookies. Do come in.''

Bendell grinned at the rest of the patrol and looked back to the older couple. ''Gee, we really appreciate it, but we really don't want to be a bother. If we could just—''

Interrupting, the old man grumbled. ''Nonsense, I fought in the Pacific in the big war, and I lost a brother to the Nazis in North Africa. We'd be damn proud to have you in our house. Now git in here 'fore you're spotted!''

The entire team shyly removed their berets and entered the house, carefully wiping their shoes and clothing off first.

Grabbing Bendell's arm, the old man led them into the family room around the corner and continued. ''You boys wannna watch Johnny Carson? We'll move the TV in here so nobody can see you through the windows.''

Bendell grinned broadly, "Thanks, sir, but not necessary. The Third Infantry won't look for us here. They can't. Your house is outside the Camp A.O. Hill boundary—where we're not allowed to be."

The old man laughed and slapped his leg. "Hee, hee, yes siree!"

Bendell replied, "Actually, it's okay, though. In Special Forces we are taught to fight unconventionally and use our initiative. As guerrilla fighters, we're also trained to rely on civilians for assistance."

The little boy said, "Man, I don't believe it. Real Green Berets!"

At the same time the woman, who had disappeared into the kitchen, reappeared, pushing a serving cart with a large pot of coffee, eight cups, and two bowls of cookies on it.

Smiling sweetly, she asked, "Coffee anyone?"

The dirt road had now become a miniature Mississippi, with mud and water everywhere. A lightning flash revealed numerous Third Regiment soldiers trying to huddle under their ponchos and stay dry.

The now worn-out captain turned to the first sergeant and grumbled, "Fuckin' snake eaters. How did we lose 'em? All right, Top . . . set up a perimeter and let's get some patrols out. Have somebody get a fire goin'. I want some coffee."

Knowing his grin couldn't be seen in the rain and darkness, the old noncom replied, "Sorry, sir, no coffee. The last of our coffee got blown all over the CP by one of their artillery simulators."

The company commander's fury now reached the boiling point as he slammed his steel pot in the mud. "Motherfuckin' snake eater cocksuckers!"

... 3 ...

TET '68

Bullets impacted all around the nude five-year-old Rhade
Montagnard girl. Ignoring the deafening sounds of the battle around her, she kept turning from one side to the other
to see the bodies of her dead parents. Thirty feet away,
several Montagnard men fired in all directions from a foxhole. One of them, Ksor Kok (pronounced Coke), was a
well-built man with black hair and mustache. There were
little dots tattooed on several spots on his body, and the
man, in his early twenties, wore camouflage fatigues, a
dirty bandage binding his left bicep.

He shouted to the others, "You men cover me! I must
save that girl!"

One of the men shouted, "No, Kok, FULRO needs
you!"

Angered, Kok turned on him. "She's one of our children!"

With that he burst from the foxhole, zigzagging through
the withering gunfire. In the background, various khaki-
clad North Vietnamese soldiers burst from woven bamboo
longhouses on stilts in the village of Buon Ale-A. Scoop-
ing her up in his arms, Kok rushed back to the foxhole
amid cheers and shouted warnings. Diving through the air,
he twisted his body as he sailed over the lip of the large

hole, landing on his back as machine-gun rounds cracked through the air.

Sweating, Kok tried to rise, the wind driven from him. Several Dega warriors patted him on the back. The little girl stopped crying as he lifted her chin and smiled into her eyes.

"Be brave, little one . . . you are Dega. Be brave and live," he said.

Another Dega, barefoot and wearing a black loincloth and faded Coors T-shirt, addressed Kok. "Kok, Major Doh told me to tell you that they called for reinforcements from the B-50 Special Forces headquarters."

Kok replied. "Did he speak to Americans or Yuan?"

"Yuan."

"Then no reinforcements will come," Kok went on. "The Yuan know that Buon Ale-A is FULRO's headquarters. The Vietnamese fear us . . . they want us killed."

Excited, another Montagnard pointed. "Kok, look, the NVA are pulling back!"

"They'll hit us again," Kok replied.

The T-shirted warrior said, "Major Doh said that the radio says the NVA hit cities all over Vietnam. *Beaucoup* Americans killed. Many Yuan too."

Kok frowned. "Many people celebrate Tet. The communists must have planned big surprise, and I think tonight we will get a big surprise. I'm going to go sleep for a while."

That night found Kok in another foxhole with two other warriors, Yuar and Y Thu, fighting against a vicious attack by North Vietnamese regulars. The NVA had taken most of the village and were lining captured Dega men, women, and children on a rise, then mowing them down with a machine gun. Their bodies fell backward, to be rolled into a ditch behind the rise of ground.

Frightened, Yuar asked, "Kok, why won't Ban Me Thuot send us reinforcements? We are fighting a regiment with thirty men."

Kok smiled. "Because, Yuar, we are Montagnard. If the NVA kills us, the Yuan won't have to find excuses to execute us." He paused and reloaded. "Let's die as Dega. I am a Jarai warrior, and I will die a Jarai warrior."

Yuar gulped and said proudly, "I am Jarai and will die Jarai."

Y Thu, following suit, said, "I am Rhade warrior and will die a Rhade."

"Look out!" Kok yelled as an American hand grenade bounced into their hole.

Sweat ran off Kok's face as he stared at it, then broke into a grin. He bent over and picked it up, showing the rubber band holding the handle in place. The three laughed nervously, and Kok removed the band and threw the grenade back at the NVA.

Kok said, "Stupid NVA didn't remove the rubber band." Closing his eyes, he said, "Thank you, Jesus."

"Cousin," Yuar said. "Why do always thank Jesus?"

Kok said proudly, "Because I am a Christian. Jesus protects me and will save our people someday."

Thonk! Another hand grenade landed in the bottom of the foxhole, but again the band had not been removed. And again Kok removed the band and tossed the grenade at the enemy. No sooner had Kok thrown it than a third grenade landed in the foxhole. Miraculously, it, too, had a rubber band around it. Yuar quickly removed the band and threw it. While throwing it, however, Yuar found himself staring into the face of an NVA twenty feet away, just as the soldier squeezed the trigger on a B-40 rocket launcher.

"Duck!" Yuar screamed as all three dropped to the floor of the hole just as the B-40 rocket exploded right at the lip of the foxhole.

The three were dusted with dirt and debris but were otherwise unscathed. Visibly shaken, they sat up, wiping the dirt from themselves.

Eyes wide, Kok blurted, "We are okay!"

Then simultaneously Y Thu and Yuar said, "Thank you, Jesus! Thank you, Jesus!"

Rising then, Y Thu spoke. "Maybe Jesus does protect you, Kok, but I would rather have a steel pot and a flak jacket. I'm leaving."

Also rising, Yuar started to crawl away. "Me too."

Kok looked around and shrugged and, with a sigh, also bellied out of the hole. When he'd crawled ten feet, the foxhole exploded from a direct mortar hit. Eyes bulging, Kok started crawling faster. While NVA soldiers were running, yelling, and shooting all over the village, the wiry Dega crawled past one foxhole filled with villagers and wriggled into the next with three unarmed Montagnards. The four immediately started arguing.

"Kok," one irate villager said, "get rid of the rifle. If they think we are peaceful civilians, they won't kill us!"

Kok's lips curled back over his teeth, "Shut up, coward! We are Dega. That is the only reason they want to kill us! I will at least die a man!"

The three looked up and beyond Kok, then froze in fear. Kok turned to see a grinning NVA soldier aiming an SKS rifle right between Kok's eyes. The enemy soldier stood on the hole's edge, so close that Kok watched in horror as his finger squeezed the trigger.

Whomp!

Most of the NVA's head exploded forward, sending blood, flesh, bits of skull, and brain matter all over Kok and his cohorts. Shot from behind, his body sailed forward, landing on Kok and pinning him as neatly as a Greco-Roman wrestler. Amazed that he was still among the living, Kok, completely drenched with the dead soldiers's blood, wriggled free and jumped up, smiling through a red liquid shroud.

Again the three stared in horror past Kok. Before he could react, he felt a rifle barrel shoved up against the base of his skull. The unseen enemy shoved his rifle barrel forward, pushing Kok's face all the way into the puddle of blood from the dead soldier. In the meantime another NVA bound Kok's coppery wrists behind his back. They were bound so tightly with army commo wire that both wrists started bleeding. After tying the others the NVA moved all four out of the foxhole. The fighting ceased as they and other Dega marched toward the firing squad position.

Smoke hung low over the entire area, and the acrid smell of burned gunpowder hit Kok's nose. Soaked with the dead enemy's blood and his own sweat, the Dega's muscular body had an eerie look in the moonlight and the half-light from the burning longhouses.

Kok gulped, holding his chest out and shoulders erect as he and the other twenty-nine Montagnard captives were lined up for the firing squad.

An NVA in a fairly clean khaki uniform and pith helmet fed ammo into the chamber of a Soviet RPD machine gun and sighted down the barrel at the hostages. Three more prepared to take aim with AK-47 assault rifles. Between whispered prayers, Kok looked at the rifles and wondered if he would be able to hear the tinny metallic sound of the AKs before bullets tore into his flesh. Or would he hear nothing? He pictured H'Li's smiling face, and a slight smile touched his lips.

"*Mau phai tra mau,*" hissed a North Vietnamese buck sergeant standing by the machine gun.

"What did he say, Kok?" Hip, the Dega to Kok's left, asked nervously.

"He said, 'Blood must be paid by blood,' Hip," Kok replied.

Hip gulped and said, "Kok, ask your Jesus to save us."

"What do you think I've been doing?"

The NVA cocked their weapons and aimed at the hopeless captives.

Kok yelled out defiantly, "I die proud, a Montagnard and a Christian!" Whispering, he continued, eyes closed. "Our Father, who art in heaven, hallowed be thy name, thy kingdom come, thy—"

Kok was interrupted by the shout of an NVA officer. *"Khong!"*

All the members of the firing squad looked over at the speaker, whose arms were held up. They relaxed their arms and lowered their weapons. Kok's frame dropped in relief, and he choked back tears.

The officer continued, "Don't shoot them! We need prisoners for labor and current intelligence! Blindfold them and tie them together!"

Hip, drenched with sweat, turned to face Kok, who was grinning triumphantly.

"You must tell me about this Jesus," Hip said.

"He protects me."

"Always?"

Smiling, Kok said, "Always . . . ugh!"

Kok dropped to his knees, having been smashed in the solar plexus by the butt of an NVA's rifle. The wind driven from him, Kok fought against the panicky feeling until he was able to breathe again. The soldier grabbed Kok's hair and raised his head, spitting into the Dega hero's eyes.

"Moi!" The soldier sneered after shouting the word, which loosely translates to the word *nigger* in English, then walked away.

Kok struggled to his feet as Hip whispered, "Are you okay?"

"Yes, but we must live and escape." Kok grunted. "We must help our people."

"But how can we help our people against these bastards?" Hip queried.

"Americans," Kok replied. "Americans."

... 4 ...

PLAYING WAR

A black-pajamaed sergeant slapped another, who was lying on the ground next to him and had begun to snore. Startled, the sleeper jumped up in a fighting stance, his green beret flying off his face—a face that started to turn beet red as the other team members all chuckled quietly at him.

Embarrassed, he said, "Fuck you, guys. No offense, Lieutenant."

"None taken, Sergeant." Bendell laughed with the rest. "You were just snoring kind of loud."

"Kind of loud," said another NCO. "Shit, he's louder than my old lady's pussy farts. 'Cept his breath smells about the same."

Everybody laughed as the sleeper responded. "I hope you get blown away in 'Nam while I'm humpin' yer old lady, you asshole."

"Well, if you want some of that overused pussy, man . . ." came the reply.

The sleeper grinned, "Well, it probably ain't bad once I get past the used part, ha ha."

Surrounded by dark green ivy and numerous vines, Bendell rolled on his back and blew cigarette smoke skyward, watching cloud shapes through the holes in the Virginia hardwood forest cover. Next to him, Staff Sergeant

Bobby Stewart played an abbreviated version of mumblety-peg with Sergeant First Class Jim Hale.

Hale said to the second lieutenant, "Hey, Thieu-uy, with all the miles we're puttin' in, lean your legs up against that tree trunk while yer relaxin'. Gets the blood flowing good, rejuvenates yer legs."

"Thanks Sergeant Hale," Bendell replied.

Grinning, the blond, balding sergeant brushed his stripes and then his head. "I told you: old man . . . many stripes . . . hair growing thin . . . many years . . . you listen, I teach you."

"That's right Lieutenant," Bobby Stewart chimed in. "We told you, yer under our wing. We're gonna teach ya."

"Why me?" Bendell asked.

"Simple, sir. Yer gung ho, but you listen to yer NCOs. You don't act like yer shit don't stink, so we decided to take ya under our wing and teach ya—"

Jim Hale interrupted. "In Special Forces you've got the smartest and best NCOs in any army in the world—some even have master's degrees. Just remember to use us to make you look good and accomplish your mission, and don't ever tell an SF NCO how to do his job and you'll be a fuckin' war hero . . . and a good officer that we don't mind followin'."

"That's why everybody learned the three rules for survival, sir," Bobby added.

"What's that?" Bendell asked.

Jim grinned as Bobby started to answer, "Simple, Thieu-uy. Number one, never piss against a head wind; number two, don't ever call Batman a pussy; and, number three, don't ever fuck with Special Forces."

Jim held up his hand for silence as a squirrel chattered. "Quiet! Cigarettes out!" he whispered loudly. "There's Richardson's signal, they're comin'!"

Quickly, quietly, and efficiently, all the team members grabbed their weapons and rolled into hiding positions in the thick foliage. All eyes focused on the wooded hillside across the ravine.

The point patrol showed up from the Third Infantry Regiment company on the FTX (field training exercise). Slowly, carefully, they made their way up the hillside, suspiciously eyeing the colored leaflets tacked to the trees at the hill's crest. Soon the rest of the company came into view. From their huffing and puffing, it was obvious that many of the soldiers had spent more time performing precision drill and ceremony, doing drop jobs at Arlington Cemetery or guarding places such as the Tomb of the Unknown Soldier than humping the boonies.

Bendell grinned, watching the company commander huff and puff, figuring a lot of this was from rage and frustration. The captain finally made it close to the line of leaflets. Several groups of soldiers, including the lieutenant, gathered around the leaflets. Chuckles and snickers were even audible to Bendell's team members.

The CO bellowed at the lieutenant, "Well, what's it say, Lieutenant?"

Fighting a smirk, the young XO responded, "Well, sir, it's a leaflet printed by the aggressors."

"Okay, okay, read it, dammit!"

The lieutenant, still trying hard to suppress his laughter, responded, "Yes, sir! It says, 'Why do you imperialists come to our land and kill all our people while families are left alone and lonely, especially you, Captain . . . uh, sir, it gives your full name, serial number, and home address."

The captain growled. "Fuckin' green beanies . . . yeah, go on, Lieutenant. Keep reading."

The lieutenant, still nearly laughing, went on. "Yes, sir, it says, 'You know, Dai-uy, your wife, Victoria, was very lonely and really enjoyed it when we gang-banged her, and, boy, does she ever give number-one blowjobs!' It's signed, 'Vietcong.' "

Laughter broke out throughout the company, some soldiers falling on the ground holding their sides. Half of Bendell's team had to muffle their laughter in their berets as they watched the captain go through color changes like a hyperactive chameleon.

Storming toward the leaflet, he screamed, "What! Lemme see that!"

What the enraged officer did not see were the two wires taped to the back of the leaflet with olive-drab tape. He yanked it off the tree angrily, and a pop, hiss, and whistle began as thick green smoke sprewed out from the hidden smoke grenade and the whistle from the artillery simulator sounded an alarm. The captain dived just as the simulator exploded, sending dirt and leaves flying for fifteen feet.

A major, wearing a white arm band and carrying a note-book, walked over and grinned at the captain as he rose to his feet.

A short stubble of red hair showed under his helmet liner as the major, a referee, spoke to the commanding officer, "Captain, you and these eight men were killed by those booby traps. Those two over there would be wounded and must be medevaced."

Frustrated, the captain fairly pleaded, "But, Sir! Please? I. . . ."

"You're dead, Captain. Where's your XO? He's in command."

"Over here, sir!" the lieutenant yelled.

Smiling, the redheaded field grade said, "You're the CO now. Carry on, Lieutenant."

"Yes, sir." The Lieutenant beamed and turned away.

The captain, furious, rolled up the leaflet and threw it down. "Fuckin' Green Berets!"

He kicked a tree and started hopping around in pain, and the woods rang with laughter.

Bendell and his team low-crawled away, laughing heartily. Over the opposite hilltop they stood up and lit cigarettes and cigars.

Bendell said, "Okay, we need to hump over to the mock

VC village and get in our hiding places. They'll be there shortly.''

Sergeant Hale jumped in. ''All right you mother-humpers. Ya heard the leftenant; You two take point. Let's book it.''

With economy of movement and virtually no sound, each man fell into his own place naturally. With a two-man point fifty meters ahead, they moved rapidly through the woods, soon emerging in a clearing filled with bamboo huts, a hay pile, a pigpen, and a village cookfire in the center. Another NCO in black pajamas squatted Vietnamese style by the fire, drinking coffee from a smoke-blackened Army canteen cup. As the men walked up, he saluted Bendell, who returned it and handed a flashlight to each man.

Bendell pointed to a bush outside the village, ''Okay, I'm gonna use that entrance under the bush and I'll crawl down here and wait under the campfire. Those of you going into the tunnels, don't forget to watch for rattlers. They're supposed to find us, so don't hide too good.''

Bobby Stewart added, ''Keep yer ass covered too. We just made fools of 'em again and they're pissed I guaran-fuckin'-tee it.''

The small team dispersed. One reached into the hay pile, opened a trapdoor, and climbed inside. Another kicked open a trapdoor under the muck in the pigpen and disappeared down into the ground. Walking into a bamboo hut, one sergeant boosted another up onto the thatched roof, lifted a trapdoor out of the thatching, and disappeared inside, while the first sergeant opened a hidden door and disappeared into the woven bamboo wall.

Walking to the wood's edge, Bendell grabbed a branch and pulled as the whole bush, mounted on a wooden door, slid away, exposing a tunnel entrance. Bendell sat there, legs dangling in the hole, cigarette between his lips, until he heard the squirrel-chatter signal. He dropped into the tunnel and the bush slid back into place.

The entire mock Vietcong village was honeycombed by a network of tunnels made up of culvert pipes buried ten feet underground. Lieutenant Bendell now faced three such tunnels and shined his light down each, nervously looking for the ever-present rattlesnakes Team Sergeant Mike Holland had warned them about. He headed down the tunnel that went to the village cook-fire exit. He would wait a few feet back from the cook-fire entrance until they found the steelplated trapdoor under the cook fire and slid it back to send some brave "tunnel rat" volunteer down with a flashlight and a weapon filled with blanks.

The young officer inched forward on his belly, knowing the cook-fire entrance was just now beyond the beam of his flashlight. Stopping often to catch his breath and to nurse his sore elbows and knees, he began hearing muffled noises from other tunnels as, one by one, his team members were discovered.

Fighting claustrophobia, he crawled on, arms trembling from the exertion. Sweat ran into his eyes and his mouth, and his body ached everywhere. But now the entrance was just ahead, with three other tunnels jutting off at the apex. He saw what looked to be three spent smoke or CS (tear gas) grenades, thrown in previously by an overzealous platoon leader or platoon sergeant to flush out the Fort Bragg–grown VC.

Lieutenant Bendell lay in the choking hot culvert tunnel. He shook and sweated with exertion and thought about each foot of dirt above him. Trying to fight back panic, he pictured all the dirt caving in on him. He could hear his heart banging in his ears as he thought about a five-foot timber rattler crawling up behind him, between his legs, and biting his groin. He visualized the vengeful Third Infantry captain grinning down the hole under the village cook fire, dropping an HE (high-explosive) grenade into the narrow, gaping tunnel entrance. He fought back all of these thoughts and decided to make one final try for the last fifteen feet and then rest until captured. He squirmed forward down the narrow pipe for fifteen more feet . . . and then it happened.

He had crashed through an invisible wall . . . into a void filled with gas. His face felt as if he had thrust it into a roaring campfire. His tongue, throat, and lungs burned as if he were inhaling a blowtorch. Blisters and red marks started breaking out on the young lieutenant's face. He squelched a whimper of fear and struggled to crawl backward, but his elbows and sides wouldn't work in the narrow confines of the tunnel.

In the blink of an eye Bendell thought, *Oh, God, I'm burning up. I'm going to die! Don't panic! Don't inhale! Don't inhale! Back up . . . hook your toes in the ripples of the pipe and pull. Push back with your hands!*

He started backing up, but the panic—no, hear hysteria—kept fighting to control his mind. His lungs were ready to burst. He knew he had to crawl backward even faster. Finally summoning all his courage, he carefully inhaled. Fresh air . . . no gas . . . still crawling backward, he started to gulp in deep breaths of the stale, hot, dank, but nongaseous air.

"Oh, thank you, God," he sobbed, "please get me out of this tunnel."

Bendell rolled on his back and panted. Tears streamed out of his eyes and felt like molten lava as they cascaded down his cheeks and temples. Staring at the top of the culvert, six inches above his blistered face, he was now too exhausted and in too much pain to feel claustrophobic. He worried about going into shock and tried to elevate his legs, but the culvert was too confining.

I'm no Green Beret, the young officer thought to himself. *I'm scared shitless. I'm a fucking phony.*

Bendell, thinking only of survival, rolled over and started inching backward again. He was determined not to die in this. He thought back to classes at Infantry OCS. He tried to recall the symptoms for nerve gas and mustard gas and wondered if that's what had invaded his body. He started retching, feeling as if he were vomiting razor blades and hot coals.

Don Bendell had joined the Army as a private a year and a half earlier, a week after barely graduating from high school. He was a loser . . . a class clown with no self-esteem, the child of a broken marriage. He was an alcoholic by the age of fifteen, had been smoking a pack of cigarettes a day by the age of twelve. The Army had changed all that. Still in the reception station, with less than a week in the Army, he had volunteered for Vietnam, Infantry OCS, Jump School, Special Forces (the Green Berets), and Ranger training. The Army was glad to oblige. OCS had changed him into a winner; he now had self-confidence. Thanks to Barry Sadler's song and John Wayne's movie, people asked for his autograph and bought him drinks . . . a real mistake with an alcoholic. Don felt like one of the elite—not only a Green Beret but also one of their leaders.

Unfortunately, right now he couldn't really focus on being a winner. He was worried about dying in a freak training accident on a near deserted Army post in Virginia, Camp A.P. Hill. He wanted to face the Vietcong and his own fears. He wanted to win a Congressional Medal of Honor and be loved and revered by one and all. He thought of these things. He thought back two years, to when he and his buddies had stood on Turkeyfoot Golf Course and thrown apples at passing cars on U.S. Highway 619. He thought of how far he had come, and that if he was going to die, it would be in Vietnam, saving his men and accomplishing his mission.

Every soldier complains about boring repetitious training. Few realize that we only learn in two ways—either by shock or by repetition.

Any solid NCO or officer who has led men knows that in battle he is calm. The only thoughts that come are the repetitious things he learned during training. The fear comes later.

Like other soldiers who had been through it before, Lieutenant Bendell had gone through CBR (chemical-biological-radiological) training in Basic, AIT (advanced infantry training), and OCS. He had entered a small building (the gashouse) with his fellow trainees wearing an Army field protective mask. Each walked through the CS gas–filled room and stopped at the end; removed his mask; saluted the training NCO; recited his name, rank, and serial number, and then ran from the building, eyes burning, gasping for air.

This repetitive training had saved Don's life. Now crawling backward an inch at a time, the main danger past, he had to fight the fear. He could not let himself think negative thoughts. He would worry about the extent of his injuries when he got out of the tunnel.

Light! Daylight! Little cracks of daylight shot down from above but Bendell couldn't see them. It was then that he realized he was blinded, but he could sense the fresh air. He emerged from the tunnel seconds later, seeing only a fuzzy brightness.

Crawling, the lieutenant located a log, placed his feet on it, and rolled on his back. Reaching down into a side pocket in his black pajama pants, he felt a smoke grenade and pulled it out.

Pulling the pin, he dropped it and yelled, "Medic! Medic!"

The young Green Beret officer smiled as he heard voices approaching. He fainted.

By the time his team had assembled around him, he was able to see slightly. The medic applied salve to Bendell's bright red and blistered face and hands. Numerous emergency calls had been made, and already a CBN Team (chemical-biological-nuclear) from the Pentagon was boarding a HUIB helicopter and headed for Camp A.P. Hill, Virginia.

A few hours later Lieutenant Bendell, still in his contaminated black pajamas, wearing a protective mask, plastic gloves, mask, and coveralls, and armed with a special instrument to test the contaminated spot in the tunnels, crawled back inside. The CBN team had asked him to get an air sample in the exact spot in which he'd been burned. He also checked the three grenades—two were smoke, one was gas. This time, wearing the mask, he went on to the cook-fire exit and crawled out. Emerging in the sunlight, he looked at the gauge on the instrument he carried. The needle was exactly on the line between the red and amber colors In the red it said MUSTARD GAS. He felt like a hot branding iron was caught on the right side of his tongue.

The three CBN team members examined and discussed the grenade Bendell brought out.

One of them, a major, walked over, shaking his head. "You talk about freak accidents, Lieutenant," he said. "That was an experimental grenade you brought out. It's classified. We have no idea how anybody could have gotten their hands on it, much less used it on an FTX. Apparently it had been in the tunnel a good while before you entered. You're lucky."

Bendell smiled and winced, "Yes, sir, I feel lucky as shit right now."

The major laughed.

... 5 ...

DEFIANCE

Kok felt leeches slithering up his legs, knowing others were already attached to his calves and thighs, swollen tenfold from sucking his blood.

Hands bound behind them and tied neck to neck with commo wire, Kok, Hip, and the other villagers were forced down a jungle trail. Fear in their eyes, they stared at the bodies of dead Americans, Vietnamese, and Montagnards, hung in trees along side the path. Exhausted, they were forced on, mile after mile.

Hip, behind Kok, whispered, "Kok, where are we?"

Kok whispered back, "Somewhere west of Ban Me Thuot! I think somewhere near Dalat . . . ooh!"

The butt of an AK-47 slammed into Kok's gut and he stumbled to one knee, commo wire jerking tight on his throat. He gritted his teeth in pain as he stared daggers into the face of the grinning NVA guard.

"Shut up, *moi*." He sneered. "Scared, aren't you?"

Kok twisted his mouth in controlled fury and spit into the NVA soldier's grinning face. Wiping the spittle off, the enraged guard stopped the prisoners and viciously shoved his Soviet assault rifle under the Dega hero's chin and cocked it. His sadistic leer reappeared as Kok broke into a sweat. But, screwing up his courage, Kok spit into his tormentor's face again.

Wiping the spit, the guard screamed, *"Choi oi! Choi Duc oi!"*

He started to pull the trigger but was stopped by a scream from his commanding officer. *"Khong! Linh! Linh! Lai-de! Lai-de mau!"*

Shaking with rage, the soldier looked at his commander, lowered his weapon, and whispered to Kok, "Someday I will kill you, nigger."

Smiling defiantly, Kok replied, "No, yellow nigger, I will kill you."

"Linh! Lai-de mau!" the NVA officer screamed.

The guard ran over and bent in subservience as the officer beat him across his back with a bamboo club, screaming all the while.

Hip whispered to Kok, "We need to find more Americans who can help us . . . fast."

... 6 ...

THE BIG RIFLE RANGE
ACROSS THE POND

Bendell, in jungle fatigues, now wearing a silver bar on the Fifth Group flash on his beret, entered the office door. Don reported to a graying, slightly overweight lieutenant colonel seated behind a desk.

At rigid attention, Bendell said, "Sir, Lieutenant Bendell reports!"

Returning the salute, the older officer extended his hand for a shake. "At ease, Bendell, relax. Welcome to Kontum, to B-24."

Smiling, Bendell said, "Thanks, sir. I'm glad I finally made it to the Fifth Group."

"Well, you won't feel that way long."

Bendell frowned.

The colonel continued. "Anyway, congratulations on your promotion to first lieutenant."

"Thanks, Colonel."

Walking to a big wall map, the paunchy field grade pointed at a spot along the border of Laos and continued. "You're being assigned to an A-team, A-242 at Dak Pek, right here, as XO/CA-PO." So Bendell was to be executive officer of civil affairs and psychological operations.

Grinning broadly, Bendell replied, "Fuckin' A, sir. I'm ready to go."

"As you can see," the lieutenant colonel continued,

"the camp sits right on the Ho Chi Minh Trail, just a few miles from Laos. In the northwestern corner of II Corps. Actually, Dak Pek's the most isolated American unit in all of Vietnam.''

Still grinning and obviously excited, Bendell replied, "That's great, Colonel! Will I be working with Yards?"

"Oh, yes," the senior officer replied. "Primarily with the Jeh tribe of Montagnard, but there are some Sedang and Halang people there. The Jeh is one of the most primitive tribes in Vietnam." The CO continued. "Now, you know the Montagnards and Vietnamese don't get along?"

"I've heard, sir," Don replied.

"Well, just do your job and don't get between them, and especially stay away from FULRO. You've heard of it?"

"Yes, sir, I've heard," Bendell said. "It's a supersecret Montagnard movement that wants to overthrow the Saigon government and take back the Central Highlands, right?"

"Essentially," the colonel replied. "So stay away from them."

"Yes, sir."

The lieutenant colonel stuck out his hand, and the two shook again.

"Again, welcome aboard, son," the lieutenant colonel said. "There's a chopper leaving for Dak Pek at 1300 hours. Be on it."

"Yes, sir. Thank you."

... 7 ...

POW CAMP

A banded krait slithered through the dense jungle under-growth. His bite, which is neurohematoxic and affects both the nervous and circulatory systems, is one of the world's deadliest. He glided along the edge of the crudely made bamboo stocks a scant three inches below the bare feet of the now waking prisoners, Kok and Hip. The serpent slithered into the dense green carpeting as Kok sat up and tried to massage circulation back into his legs. Hip held his stomach as he looked down the line of prisoners on both sides. Two NVA guards knelt in front of a cook fire.

"I cannot live anymore just eating one potato a day, Kok," Hip complained.

"Me, too, Hip," Kok replied, "My stomach hurts bad all the time."

Kok rubbed the fresh pink bullet-graze scar on his left arm. When captured, Kok had been wearing a large ban-dage on it but removed it after his first week of captivity.

Hip inquired, "Why haven't they asked about your wound from Pleiku?"

"I don't know," Kok answered, "Why haven't they asked about FULRO? They know Buon Ale-A was our headquarters. Maybe they don't want to treat us too badly. I heard that they tried to get Y Bham to agree not to in-terfere with their war, and made him promises."

"What do you suppose he told them?"

Kok laughed. "Have you ever seen any Vietnamese, North or South, that we can trust?"

"I wish they would turn us loose."

"Me, too, Hip. I wonder if my wife has had our baby yet."

"What village is she from, Cheo Reo?" Hip asked.

"Oh, no, not my village," Kok replied. "She is not Jarai; she is a Rhade from Ban Me Thuot."

Kok stared at the thick green jungle canopy overhead as he thought of H'Li, his smiling young wife. He pictured a scene from a few years earlier about which she had told him. She had been eighteen, headstrong, and in love.

H'Li's mother and father had been standing just outside the door of the longhouse, arguing with the young girl.

"Girl, you are crazy!" Her father said, "All you know is that he is somewhere in Cambodia. You can't even find him, and the jungle is treacherous and full of enemies!"

"I don't care!" H'Li shouted stubbornly. "I must find him! He is my man!"

"H'Li," her father continued, "you are being stupid and stubborn. Nobody knows where FULRO headquarters is, but I do know it's hundreds of miles from here."

H'Li stomped her foot angrily. "I don't care. I love Kok and will find him!"

Her father angrily replied, "No!" Then he turned and walked away.

Tears in her eyes, H'Li ran in the door.

That night H'Li met her two girlfriends near the jungle's edge.

"You two don't have to go," H'Li said.

One friend said, "You are our friend H'Li. We will go."

The other said, "Besides, our men are with Kok. We go."

"Okay." H'Li went on. "First we will go and wait

outside Ban Don and hide all day. At night we cross the Sar Pok. Let's go.''

All three giggled, patted one another on the backs, and ran into the jungle.

A few days later the three girls were walking behind a FULRO warrior who was their guide. They crossed a river, spotting movement on the far shore. The guide motioned them down. In the dense jungle undergrowth they saw glimpses of NVA soldier's legs. The guide signaled them forward, and they emerged into a small clearing, in which several cook fires burned.

Whispering, their guide said, "They are nearby still. Come, we must move fast.''

The three disappeared into the dense green wall.

Three days later the three love-struck young women were turned over to another guide, who had an elephant with a platform on top to ride on. They were relieved to know that they could ride for the rest of the long journey.

Kok remembered kneeling by a stream washing his clothes at the FULRO headquarters in Mondulkiri Province in Cambodia when a very excited Dega burst from the jungle.

Yelling excitedly, the Montagnard said, "Kok! Kok! Come quick! Your wife is here!''

Kok stood, dropping his clothes. "My wife? I don't have a wife!''

"Yes, you do! She's here. Come quick!''

With that, the other Dega disappeared down the jungle path. Leaving his clothes, a now totally perplexed Kok followed after him.

As he came into view of the buildings that made up the headquarters complex for FULRO, H'Li was just climbing down from the box atop the elephant. Turning, she spotted Kok. They ran to each other and stopped, both embarrassed and unsure of how to act or what to do.

Kok spoke excitedly. "H'Li, what are you doing? Why are you here? Are you crazy?!"

Smiling coyly, she kicked her bare toes into the dust and spoke. "I come to my man."

Kok replied quickly, "But, H'Li, you . . . it's dangerous! Oh, boy . . . you don't have any cousins or family here!"

Beaming, she responded, "I did not come through jungle filled with enemies for many days to be with family. *You* are my family. I came to be with you, Kok—forever."

"Oh, no! Oh, my!" Kok said, almost on the verge of a nervous breakdown. "But where will you sleep? You've no friends here."

"I will sleep and live with you," she said, her eyes flirting.

By this time, Kok was so shook up, he could hardly speak, but he replied, "Oh, boy! Oh, my! H'Li, tomorrow we will get married, okay?"

Smiling, H'Li said, "Good." Then she turned to retrieve her small satchel of belongings from the elephant.

Kok was shaken back to reality by the sound of the NVA soldiers unlocking and releasing the leg stocks on the fourteen other prisoners, then those on Hip and Kok. He was concerned because there were more guards than usual, and the commanding officer was also there, pistol drawn. The concern turned to relief and then elation as the officer pointed east down the jungle road.

He spoke sharply. *"Ong ay di au Ban Me Thuot! Di mau, moi!"*

There was a murmur among the prisoners as Hip asked, "What did he say, Kok?"

Smiling broadly, Kok said, "I don't know why, but they're releasing us. He said to go that way to Ban Me Thuot. He also said 'Go fast, niggers!' This time I won't argue. Let's go."

Amazed, tears in their eyes, the sixteen Dega prisoners walked, then trotted, then ran down the off shoot road from the Ho Chi Minh Trail. Passing the numerous bodies still hanging in the trees, tears of joy ran down their cheeks.

Hip asked excitedly, "Kok, why did they let us go?"

"I don't understand."

Smiling, Hip said, "I do. Your prayers."

All holding their pained stomachs, they simultaneously broke into a run and near sprinted for a mile before falling in a tumble of exhausted euphoria along the trail. Recapturing their breath, the group split up and gathered fruit, insects, roots, and grubs from the surrounding jungle. Within half an hour they were again on the move, stuffing themselves and walking briskly eastward.

Kok turned to Hip, who was swallowing a mouthful of maggots, and said firmly, "Hip, I will tell you one thing that I swear. I will never, ever be captured again!"

...8...

A BEGINNING

A formation of three buzzing flies hovered and zoomed over the blowing grass of the Kontum helipad, fighting against the powerful downblast from rotors on the HUID warming helicopter. One by one they flew into the Huey's interior and buzzed around the short plywood coffin, attracted by the smell of the decaying corpse within. Two sergeants in cleaned and pressed jungle fatigues, berets tucked in their fatigues' cargo pockets, finished placing six female Vietnamese passengers and the coffin in the chopper. One sergeant grabbed his nose. Frowning, he said, "C'mon, man, that fuckin' Yard is starting to get ripe."

Bent over, the two ran from the revving aircraft and waved at a third Special Forces sergeant, a stocky blond kid with a warm boyish smile. Lieutenant Bendell walked to the Huey, exchanging salutes with the blond buck sergeant, Don Willians.

"Where ya' goin', Lieutenant?" Don Williams hollered above the rotor noise.

"A-242, Dak Pek, new CA/PO-XO!" Bendell replied.

The Huey's engines revved, almost blowing their berets off. They each quickly jammed on their berets.

With a big smile the young sergeant stuck out his hand.

"Hey, welcome aboard, sir!" Williams said. "I'm Don

Williams, assistant commo man at Dak Pek. Call me
Commo Willy . . . everybody does!''

They jumped on board, and the aircraft immediately
creaked, groaned, and, with a loud whine, buzzed skyward. Bendell liked Commo Willy's smile and figured
there was at least one good man on his new team.

Commo Willy looked across at Bendell, seated on the
plywood coffin next to two of the whores. He looked at
the shiny silver bar on the flash of the lieutenant's beret.
He thought back to the last lieutenant in Bendell's job at
Dak Pek. He had taken a claymore pellet right between
the running lights. He thought back to the lieutenant before that, who also had taken a 7.62-mm bullet between
the eyes. He grinned to himself and looked out the chopper door as he wondered where this tall, slender lieutenant
would get shot. He thought of his own survival.

Commo Willy was a survivor. He had spent twenty-four
months in Vietnam, first with the First Air Cav Division
and then with the Fifth Special Forces Group. He wanted
to prove to himself, his mom, and his friends that there
was not a jinx on his family; so far, every male member
had been killed in war, except Commo Willy.

Don Bendell looked down below at the emerald-green
carpet of triple-canopy jungle and the thin blue ribbon of
the Dak Pek River, snaking its way northward along the
now overgrown Highway 14.

He yelled at Commo Willy, "Ya know, except for the
pockmarks from B-52 strikes, this is a fuckin' beautiful
country!''

Commo Willy shook his head affirmatively and pointed
down, yelling, "Just wait till you get down in that jungle.
There's waterfalls down the mountainside, all kinds of
beautiful flowers. A lot of the falls aren't even on the
map.''

Bendell looked at steep green mountains in every direction. Looking west, he spotted the A-camps at Ben Het and then Dak Seang. Before long, they passed the ruins of the A-camp at Dak Sut. He looked up at one of the whores sitting on a canvas bag marked U.S. MAIL.

He looked at her long, shiny silk pants and purple silk dress, slit to the waist. He made a mental note to learn what this peculiar but beautiful outfit was called. All Vietnamese women seemed to wear one.

Shiny black hair cascaded all the way to her waist. Her slender fingers bore several beautiful rings; he looked at her gorgeous slanted eyes and wondered what mysteries of the Orient were hidden behind them.

Noticing his stare, she dispelled all mystery and myth when she gave him a gold-toothed smile and with a grating voice said, "Hey, Trung-uy, you want I give you number-one blow job? Make you come *beaucoup*, okay?"

Bendell shook his head no and turned, laughing at himself and his romantic thoughts.

In another quarter hour the Huey passed between two tall mountains and emerged in a huge valley encircled by tall, steep jungle-covered mountains. In the middle of the valley stood their A-camp, Dak Pek. The camp was spread over eleven tiny hilltops. A small blacktopped runway ran through its center. Each hilltop was ringed with barbed wire and millions of punji stakes. The entire camp was surrounded by a giant punji stake–filled tank trap, ten feet wide and ten feet deep.

The burned-out hull of a crashed C7A Caribou cargo plane lay dead alongside the runway. Beyond the runways Bendell saw several vehicles and many oil drums at the tin-roofed camp motor pool. On the tallest hill at the northern end of the camp was the sandbag and cinder-block American team house. Below that hill to the southeast stood the two-story woven bamboo team house of the Vietnamese Special Forces team, the LLDB, or Luc Luong Bac Biet.

At the bottom of the American hill, by the camp's main

gate, stood a white, long wooden building with a red cross on its roof, the dispensary, with a large *H* in front of it to mark the camp helipad. Made of PSP, Army pierced steel planking, it was obscured by a swirl of dark green smoke from a smoke grenade.

The helicopter descended toward this welling green cloud. As skids settled onto grass, Bendell watched the green smoke, blasted by prop wash, downward and out in all directions, then upward in a near perfect circle. The engine made a loud whining whistle winding down. The two snake eaters jumped out of the open doors. Bendell and Commo Willy exchanged handshakes with a tall, big-framed first lieutenant, waiting by a stripped, beat-up jeep. Commo Willy threw two canvas mailbags and several cans of film into the vehicle.

"Brought a new Clint Eastwood Western, sir," Willy said.

The lieutenant smiled. "Super. How did yer scroungin' mission go?"

"Well, I got these six whores from some Air Force types up in Kontum. They're paid for a week in advance," he replied.

Laughing, the lieutenant replied, "That's just great, but what the hell do we want with them, Sergeant? You want half the team coming down with severe runny noses?"

Grinning, Commo Willy replied, "Hell, I don't care what you do with them, sir. I just made the trade 'cause they threw them in. I was tradin' for a sawed-off M2 carbine."

"Just terrific, out-fuckin' standing! Tell me, did you scrounge us anything worthwhile?"

"Hell, yes, Lieutenant. I have a Caribou load of food, and another one full of booze, arriving tomorrow."

"Two planeloads!" the lieutenant exclaimed. "Super! What d'you trade for all of that?"

Willy smiled. "Besides the M2, that RPD machine gun that Joe Howard captured up on Alpha Road last week."

"That's all you traded for everything?"

"Fuckin' A, Lieutenant!" Willy beamed.

"Well, good job, Sergeant," the lieutenant said. "Take the chopper crew to the team house for lunch and . . . uh . . . take these . . . uh . . . ladies up too. Maybe we can take them to Dak To and trade 'em to somebody with the Fourth Division for something."

As Commo Willy and the others moved off the lieutenant turned to Bendell. "Anyhow, welcome to Dak Pek. Call me Mike. I was XO at Dak To, but I'm getting promoted to captain shortly, so they moved me here as CO."

"Congratulations on the railroad tracks," Lieutenant Bendell replied. "How soon?"

"Few weeks. Instead of introducing you and giving you the tour, I'll let you get your feet wet and kind of leave it up to you to learn your way around."

"No problem."

Mike pointed to the coffin. "Okay, drop me off with the mail, and then take the Montagnard boy's body to his village." Pointing, he continued. "It's that one there, the first hill, Dak Jel Luk."

A few minutes later Bendell pulled up to the base of the hill that Dak Jel Luk topped. He looked at the muddy path that wound its way up the hillside, up to the wooden gate in the circling wooden stockade wall. Thousands of needle-sharp bamboo punji stakes pointed outward around the wall. The hilltop was home to several communal bamboo-woven longhouses on stilts, or maraos, and was covered with underground bunkers, trenches, and cooking fires. Other Jeh villages dotted the background on numerous other hilltops. In fact, fifteen Jeh villages surrounded Dak Pek Valley and held a Montagnard population of over eight thousand.

The five-foot-tall Montagnard interpreter, Nhual, jumped out of the passenger side. He had an intelligent and handsome face, with a streak of red in his hair from a childhood bout with malnutrition. He barked orders to a couple of nearby loincloth-clad villagers, who unloaded the coffin from the back of the jeep and started up the path with it. Don and Nhual followed the village men.

"So, Nhual," Bendell asked, "are you the head interpreter for Dak Pek?"

"Yes, I am, Trung-uy," the stocky Jeh replied. "There's three more—Suat, and then Tuan and Tieh."

"All Jeh?" Bendell queried.

"Tuan is Sedang. The rest of us are Jeh," Nhual said, then continued. "Trung-uy, you know this child was the son of the village chief and he might not understand his death. He might be very angry."

"Oh, shit," the lieutenant exclaimed. "What did the child die of?"

"I don't know," Nhual said. "My people act ignorant sometimes. Their child gets sick. They wait long time and take him to your medics when he is almost dead. Then he dies and they blame Americans for not curing him. Damn Montagnards! They are dumb about nutrition too. You'll see many children with swollen feet and bellies, from beriberi and malnutrition." Pointing at his red streak, he concluded, "That is why many of us have red streaks or red hair."

"You seem to know a lot about medicine, Nhual," Bendell said. "You a medic too?"

Nhual grinned. "No, I try to know a little about everything."

The two entered the gate through the solid wooden stockade wall. Bendell was reminded of every cavalry fort in every Western he had seen as a child. They stopped just inside the gate, approached by all the villagers, led by the chief and his wife. The women were bare-breasted and wore only the customary *atok*, the ankle-length black silk wraparound skirt. The men wore black loincloths, and several wore tan or black shirts. Most were armed with M1 carbines; the rest carried long spears, knives, and crossbows.

The lanky young officer bent over the plywood coffin and, slinging his CAR-15 rifle over his shoulder, he pried the coffin lid off with his K-bar knife and lifted out the boy's green-plastic-wrapped corpse. Cradling the body in his arms, he walked toward the village chief.

"Xin loi," Bendell said meekly.

Quietly Nhual said, "Don't speak Vietnamese, Trung-uy. They don't speak it and will not like you for speaking it."

As the two reached the chief, as if at a silent signal, two dozen guns were cocked and aimed at Bendell simultaneously. Sweating, Bendell licked his lips. Staring into the chief's eyes, but speaking to Nhual, he said, "Nhual, tell him I am very sorry."

Nhual whispered, "There is no word in Jeh for sorry, Trung-uy."

"Then tell him his son is dead."

Nhual said, *"Kon mi kochiat oi."*

The wife started wailing. The chief's face screwed up in anger, and he said bitterly, *"Ek!"* Then, after a pause, he said. *"Sa ai?"*

Bendell whispered, "What did he say?"

"He said, 'Shit!' " Nhual replied. "Then he asked 'Why?' "

The young Green Beret could feel his heart pounding like a B-52 strike in his temples, ears, and the sides of his neck. He could barely swallow but felt it was important not to show fear.

Working up his courage, he spoke firmly to Nhual, not letting his eyes stray from the village chief, "Nhual, tell the chief that we fucked up . . . period!"

Nhual spoke to the chief. *"Mil-ken dei pi khet!"*

Bendell and the much shorter village leader stared at each other in silence for several seconds. The chief reached out and took the child's body, and the guns were immediately lowered. The tension simply disappeared. A hand-carved log casket was brought forth and the child's body placed inside.

The chief finally broke his silence, addressing Don. *"Lih-tonang au, mi huit nhiah. Au nhin lih-tonang . . . Bal hay cha konei."*

Nhual smiled broadly and said, "He says you have a friend for life."

"What did he say, exactly, Nhual?" Bendell asked.

Nhual replied, "He said he respected the lieutenant, and you, him, and me will eat rat and drink rice wine together."

Half sarcastically, Bendell said, "Tell him that's number-one . . . just great!"

Looking at the chief, Nhual said, *"Yuyh liam jei!"*

Breaking into a grin, the chief led Bendell and Nhual toward his bunker. The young officer noticed villagers tearing the coffin apart and carrying pieces off to their bunkers.

"Trung-uy," Nhual said, "my people are ignorant about modern things but are good at judging people."

"Yeah?" Bendell replied, puzzled.

Nhual went on. "In my language there are two ways to say 'we.' One is *hay*. It just means 'we.' "

"So?" Bendell said.

"When the chief said 'We will eat rat,' for 'we,' he said, *'bal hay,' "* Nhual continued.

Curious, Bendell asked, "What's that mean?"

Grinning, Nhual responded, "It means 'us people.' It means he was saying that you are also a Jeh."

Masking the emotion he was feeling, the lieutenant grinned and said, "Does that mean I gotta eat more rat?"

Laughing, Nhual said, "My people respect courage and honesty very much."

An hour later Bendell eyed the sandbagged machine-gun bunkers and mortar pits atop the Americans' hill as he and Nhual parked and entered the thirty-by-sixty-foot tin-and-sandbag-roofed team house. Inside, team members sat at a long table, drinking beer or coffee, reading their mail, and swapping gossip with the chopper crew. Mike handed Bendell a cigarette and lit it, then introduced him to the Vietnamese cook, Hazel, and the rest of the team members. A short, Italian-looking staff sergeant burst through the door and hurriedly walked up to Mike.

Speaking quickly, he said, "Lieutenant, we got trouble! The LLDB team is claiming those six whores that Commo Willy brought. They're headed this way, armed to the teeth, wearin' helmets and flak jackets."

"All of 'em?" Mike questioned.

"Every swingin' dick, Lieutenant," the Italian sergeant said.

"Everybody grab a weapon and a couple grenades, Mike snapped. "We'll meet em at the top of the driveway. Larry, grab the M-60!"

In seconds the Americans were standing side by side across the driveway adjacent to the team house.

Walking abreast, the LLDB team, armed to the teeth and wearing helmets and flak jackets, halted at the base of the hill, fifty feet below.

The LLDB, like its American counterpart, also wore green berets. They were supposedly in command of each A-camp, with the U.S. Special Forces team acting as their advisers. In most camps there was a constant power struggle between the American and Vietnamese Special Forces. One of the most important things to the Vietnamese was not losing face, so quite often, to assert authority, the LLDB would try to find ways to make their counterparts lose face.

Standing in front of the LLDB team was Mike's counterpart Trung-uy Hoe, the camp commander.

Mike yelled, "What's this all about, Trung-uy Hue?"

Hoe responded, "We want those women!"

Mike replied, "They're already paid for!"

Thieu-uy Minh, the executive officer, a big troublemaker, said to Hoe, "Let's shoot the Americans."

At the same time Mike whispered, "Lieutenant Bendell, you're gonna love this. That's your counterpart, Lieutenant Minh."

Like Clint Eastwood in *A Fistful of Dollars*, Bendell shoved a little Swisher Sweet cigarillo between his lips. He pulled his newly inscribed Zippo lighter out of his jungle fatigue pants and slowly lit the cigar while he again grinned at the inscription on the lighter: "1Lt Donald R. Bendell A-242, Dak Pek," and below it, "Let me win your hearts and your minds or I will burn down your fucking hut."

Looking up with his best man-with-no-name leer, Bendell muttered, "Oh, just great," and then yelled to Minh, *"Chiao Thieu-uy Minh, man jioi?"*

Minh grinned and yelled back, *"Da man jioi, Trung-uy!* You speak Vietnamese good."

Bendell replied, "Shoot good, too, and I'm gonna shoot you first, you little yellow fucker!"

Angrily Hoe said to Mike, "You should give us those women. We are the commanders, you are just advisers."

Quietly cocking his .45 automatic, Mike yelled back, "That's not the point, Trung-uy! Most of my men won't touch them, but it would make us lose face if we gave them to you, so we must fight!"

"I was going to make you a gift of those diseased whores," Hoe responded, "but your new lieutenant made Thieu-uy Minh lose face."

Bendell made a face but then yelled, *"Thieu-uy Minh, xin loi!* I apologize for slandering an officer of your fine and obvious bovine ancestry."

While several of the Americans chuckled, the Vietnamese LLDB team, seemingly satisfied, turned and headed back toward their elaborate, woven-bamboo team house. As they walked away and the Americans watched, still ready to shoot if need be, one of the sergeants sat down and laughed, tears streaming down his cheeks.

Another sergeant asked, "What's so funny, man?"

The laugher blurted, "*Bovine* means 'cow.' That new lieutenant called Minh a fuckin' cow, man!"

... 9 ...

A NEW IDENTITY

Kok hadn't been to Pleiku since being wounded prior to his capture at Buon Ale-A. Besides the bullet graze on his arm, a bullet actually had ricocheted straight up, cut his lip, lodged in one nostril, and had had to be removed by an American doctor in Pleiku. Now he was walking down the street in downtown Pleiku with two other Dega. A young Montagnard boy ran up to Kok.

"Are you Ksor Kok?" he asked.

Kok said, "Yes, why?"

"Come quickly!" the boy said, and led the three into an alley. He looked around nervously.

Putting one hand behind his back, Kok said, "If this is a trap—"

Interrupting, the boy said, "No! No! You must escape from Pleiku!" Seeing the puzzled look on Kok's face, he continued. "The Vietnamese are looking all over for you."

Kok said, "Me? Why?"

"The Vietnamese already publicly executed three FULRO leaders. The ARVN surrounded a FULRO force, and three hundred FULRO had to surrender. They know that our President, Y Bham Enuol, sent you here to organize and train the Bahnar tribe and others around Pleiku and Cheo Reo," the young man said. "As young as you

58

are, you are already a hero with our people, so the Viets want to find you and shoot you.''

Hand still behind his back, Kok pulled out a Walther PPK automatic and jacked a round into the chamber.

Uncocking it and tucking it in his waistband under his shirt, he said, ''Thank you. I'll get away. Don't worry.''

Running into a tree-covered yard off the alleyway, he scaled a pinkish, adobe-looking building and easily cleared the wall. He swung onto the rooftop, ran along its crest, and jumped across another alley onto another rooftop and disappeared.

A short while later Kok's uncle, a school principal, was going through student records in his office. He swatted a pesky fly, got up, and raised the window behind his desk higher. Fanning himself with a piece of cardboard, the graying Jarai teacher stepped over to a cabinet and started looking through files. He didn't hear the shadow that slipped through the open window behind his desk. Turning, he jumped and dropped papers and files at his feet, startled by the sight of Kok seated at his desk.

''Kok, what are you doing here?'' the principal asked.

''Uncle, I need your help.''

''What?''

''The Yuan are looking for me,'' Kok went on. ''I need a new name and identification papers so I can get out of Pleiku. Can you do it?''

Kok's uncle walked over to a counter and picked up a Polaroid camera. ''Smile, Nephew.''

Twenty minutes later he handed Kok his new ID and shook hands, saying, ''Pleased to meet you Mr. Siu Ton, industrious student.''

Looking at the papers and smiling, Kok said, ''Thank you.''

''What will you do now?'' the uncle asked.

Kok smiled, ''I'm having Nay Them buy me an Air Vietnam ticket to Ban Me Thuot. The Green Berets love our people. The Yuan will never expect me to go to the

Pleiku Mike Force or Special Forces C-Team headquarters. I'll fly out under their noses thanks to you.''

"Well, be very careful.''

These words echoed in Kok's mind as he stood sweating at an MP checkpoint outside the Pleiku airport two and a half hours later. His taxi had been stopped by an American MP and a Vietnamese QC. While the Vietnamese military cop went through the passenger's bags on one side of the cab, the American went through them on Kok's side. In fact, while Kok tried to hide his fear, the MP was going through his bag and was almost ready to lift the blanket at the bottom that covered his Walther PPK. If found, he would be arrested and accused of being a Vietcong. It wouldn't be long before the Viets would discover his true identity. He would then, simply and unmercifully, be tortured and then killed. The MP lifted the blanket.

Kok said, "Oh, come on, sir. I'm a student, not a VC.''

Stopping, the MP stood and smiled. "Hey, you speak English.''

"Oh, yes, I'm a student,'' Kok said. "Work part-time as interpreter for American.''

Smiling, the MP handed Kok the bag and patted him on the back. "Okay, you can go.''

"Thank you,'' Kok said excitedly.

While boarding the Air Vietnam twin-engine plane a short while later, Kok looked back and noticed a Vietnamese minister who knew him from his high-school days. The minister started pushing his way through the crowd toward the QCs as Kok boarded. He watched out the window as the plane started taxiing for takeoff. He grinned to himself as the wheels lifted off the runway, but then frowned as he realized that the authorities would be looking for him when they landed at Ban Me Thuot International Airport. Fortunately, when he landed, the authorities were only looking for Ksor Kok and not Siu Ton. He passed through with no problems.

... 10 ...

FIRST OPERATION

Standing behind the American's team house, Mike put his hand on Bendell's shoulder and pointed to the west. Bendell looked at the steep, emerald-colored mountains and looked at the four side-by-side peaks, their muddy tops trimmed away and totally devoid of jungle cover or any other greenery.

Pointing left to right, Mike said, "Those three FSBs are holding a battalion from the First Brigade, Fourth Infantry Division out of Dak To. We have two NCOs and a hundred strikers on that northwesternmost mountain, providing flank security. As a rule we don't send people out on an operation their first and last thirty days in-country, but our team is so shorthanded." He lit a Lucky Strike and continued. "I know that this is only your first day here, but I want you to go up there tomorrow to relieve one of the NCOs."

"No problem," Bendell said, lighting a cigarillo. "I came here to fight and kick ass."

Despite the outward bravado, he felt swarms of butterflies flittering in his gut, this was his first operation. He glanced down at his Zippo and read the inscription on the opposite side. In the middle was the now familiar Special Forces crest with the words DE OPPRESSO LIBER, meaning "Liberators of the Oppressed." Below that was a nasty

Peanuts cartoon, and on the lid were inscribed the words FUCK: COMMUNISM, HO CHI MINH, JOAN BAEZ, LEGS.

"Well," Mike said, chuckling, "you'll probably sit on your ass and get wet. Oh, you will get to run some patrols and ambushes to protect their flank."

"I'll go pack my rucksack and load up some magazines," Bendell said. "Where can I get some serum albumin and morphine syrettes?"

"At the dispensary," Mike replied. "See Bac-Si." Bac-Si meant "doctor" but was the nickname of all SF medics. "He'll fix you up."

"Willco," Don said, walking away. "Thanks, Mike."

He headed down the driveway next to the team house toward the dispensary. To his right was the large water tank, filled each day by a deuce-and-a-half with a tank welded on its bed, and a pump with a long hose dropped into the clear, cold Dak Poko River, which ran through the edge of the camp. Below the water tank built into the crest of the hill was the cinder-block shower room, which also had three sinks and mirrors. Next to it was the insulated bunker holding one of the two large gas-driven generators that supplied electricity for the Americans. Beyond that was the arms room, where two Montagnards, trained by Sergeant Weeks and Sergeant Challela, the weapons specialists, repaired weapons, which with a strike force of seven hundred Montagnard mercenaries, were always breaking down. Additionally the arms-room Yards would cut down, sand, and stain the stocks of M2 carbines with pistol-grip handles. Reslung, these sawed-off, modified weapons were great for trading to Air Force types for food, booze, and goodies.

Beyond the arms room, by an 81-mm mortar pit, Bendell came upon a cute seven-year-old Montagnard girl in a dirty Cleveland Browns sweatshirt. She put out her arms, smiling, wanting to be picked up. He did so, and she squeezed his neck.

"What's your name?" He asked.

"Name me—Plar," she replied.

"Well, Plar, you sure are cute. Where's your mommy and daddy?"'

"VC kill," she replied nonchalantly.

Bendell said weakly, "Oh . . ."

Across the parade ground from the LLDB team house, he turned left at the corner of a long, empty, unfinished building. He stopped dead when he almost ran into a gorgeous, raven-haired, twenty-one-year-old Jeh woman. Her long, shiny black hair hung below her waist. Unlike the older Jeh women, who had drooping breasts after years of nursing and no physical support, her bare breasts were firm, taut, and thrust out and up. Bendell could hardly look into her laughing brown eyes.

Speaking to himself as he started to go on, he said, "What a set of knockers."

Smiling beautifully, she said, "Thanks, Trung-uy, you same-same look number-one thou!"

She giggled heartily as the young officer's face turned beet red.

"I'm sorry . . . uh . . . excuse me," he said, stumbling. "You speak English."

She laughed, "It's okay . . . I glad you like. I am Ning. Hello, Plar."

Plar giggled. *"Ning, chung-li ba Plar. Ba au liem jei,* huh?"

"What did she say?" Bendell asked.

Ning chuckled. "She say that you daddy to Plar. Ask you wonderful."

Again the flustered lieutenant turned crimson and started shuffling his feet.

"Gotta go, Ning," he said. "Nice meeting you."

"Me see you more later." She smiled seductively. "You see me more later same-same."

Plar waved as Bendell walked on, still carrying her.

Montagnard men, women, and children were everywhere. There were seven hundred fighters or "strikers" with Dak Pek's force, plus their wives and children. Adding the villagers the total Dega population in the valley totalled over eight thousand. In addition, many of the twelve Vietnamese in the LLDB team had their families and relatives at Dak Pek, giving it a Vietnamese population of around one hundred. A lot of these relatives were either ARVN draft dodgers, deserters, or wanted criminals hiding out. Don and Plar passed two of those hangers-on.

Both chuckled as one spoke softly to the other as Bendell passed, carrying the dirty little cutie. *"Dung cai do hu ong-ay me . . ."*

Bendell turned furious and spoke in an angry, low voice. *"Choi oi! Loi biet ranh het ngoui Viet!"*

The two Vietnamese, red-faced and frightened, started bowing apologetically to Bendell, shocked that he had understood their put-down.

Both bowing, they said pleadingly, *"Xin loi, Trung-uy! Hai ching toi khong! Xin loi!"*

Putting on his now familiar Clint Eastwood mask, Bendell pulled out a cigarillo, slowly lit it, raised his head, and gave them a hard-core squint.

"Yeah, well, I'm not laughing, assholes," he said, blowing smoke in their faces. *"Loi khong buon cuoi, oi. Di mau, lo dit!"*

Walking on, Bendell and Plar went to the dispensary, met the medic, picked up the supplies, and left. Starting back up the driveway toward the team house at the top of the hill, Bendell heard a jeep behind him. A slender E5 driver with dark hair and a mustache stopped, and Bendell and Plar jumped in. The two soldiers shook hands.

With what sounded like a Texas accent, the sergeant said, "How ya' doin', Lieutenant? Joe Howard, team intel sergeant. You and I are bunker mates."

Bendell smiled. "You're the son of a bitch that rates the double bed, huh?"

Joe laughed. "Hey, don't bitch. You got mosquito netting."

Now Bendell laughed. "Okay, fair enough. Nice meetin' you, Sergeant Howard."

"Please call me Joe, Trung-uy. Hiya, Plar."

Plar giggled. "Hi, Trung-si Howard."

Joe stopped the jeep and grinned at Plar. "Why don't you go see if Nhual's wife has any candy or pop, okay?"

Plar's eyes lit up as she gave Bendell a kiss. Then she jumped down, running off past the water tank and shower room toward Nhual's bunker.

Bendell saw a circling chopper as Joe Howard did a U-turn and headed back toward the camp runway, down below.

The Huey was landing as the two Green Berets arrived at the runway. The American GIs, both crying, pulled the limp body of a third off the helicopter. A boy about seventeen, he had been shot in the thigh, groin, stomach, and twice in the chest.

Joe turned to Bendell. "Fourth Division just had a LRRP team shot up on that mountain."

He pointed to a jungle-covered mountain due south of the camp.

Continuing, he said, "They ran into some gooks in a bunker with an RPD machine gun."

Joe stopped the jeep and the two soldiers lit cigarettes while watching from a short distance. What was happening was obvious; the Americans had no body bags, so still crying, the two young soldiers were trying to stuff their buddy's body, shot to doll rags, into a body bag used for the shorter Vietnamese.

Bendell had long since learned to play the complete macho game and was effectively hiding the horror he felt inside. Robin Moore had written a best-seller, *The Green Berets*, and John Wayne's movie of the same name was a hit; Barry Sadler had had the hit song, "Ballad of the Green Berets." Consequently, back in the "world" in 1967 and early 1968, he and other SF troopers were celebrities. Drinks were bought for them and autographs asked for.

Bendell was often asked, "Is it true you guys are trained to kill people a hundred different ways?"

And just as often he would answer, stone-faced, "Pick a fuckin' number," throw in a pause for effect, then add, "Just don't pick number forty-seven. I'd have to take my hands out of my pockets."

Since this celebrity status had developed, an unwritten law had emerged among Special Forces troopers. They would strive to laugh at death, and outfight, outdrink, and outgross any other type of soldier, marine, sailor, or fly-boy around. The young lieutenant thought back to Fort Bragg and some of his buddies, who had learned the trick of eating a certain type of drinking glass, so they would go to bars to show off. He remembered all the grim jokes when one of them left for Vietnam.

Watching these two young Americans crying hysterically while trying to stuff their friend in the undersize bag and zip it up, the arms and legs continuously popping out, Bendell could think of no jokes or wisecracks. He could barely maintain the phony gung ho macho mask he had learned so effectively. Instead he and Joe just cleared their throats and glanced soberly at each other.

Finally, sarcastically, Joe spoke while pulling away. "Welcome to 'Nam, Lieutenant."

"I can't believe that this is still my first day at Dak Pek," Bendell replied somberly. "Can you point out Nhual's bunker? I'm supposed to eat with him and his family."

Cheering up, Joe said, "Sure, it's the first bunker in the hillside, right past our shower room. You'll love the Yards, sir."

"I already do," Bendell said.

Several hours later Bendell swallowed his last piece of meat and chased the meal with a can of beer. He glanced at Nhual's wife's large breasts swinging to and fro and thought about the fact that he had already gotten used to seeing bare tits everywhere he looked. Plar was asleep with her head on his lap, and Nhual's five-year-old daughter, Nua, was tickling her giggling three-year-old brother. Nhual's wife put water to boil on the cook fire in the center of the ten- by ten- by five-foot high underground bunker. The smoke drifted out the little chimney hole in the ceiling. A single light bulb illuminated the dirt walls, covered with pictures of American cars and cityscapes, carefully cut from magazines. Nhual picked up a guitar from the corner, tuned it, and started playing the theme song from *Bonanza*.

"Geez, Nhual," Bendell said. "You can even play a guitar?"

Nhual grinned. "Yeah, a sergeant taught me and gave me this guitar."

Smiling, Bendell said, "Well, you tell your wife the meal was great. The meat tastes a lot like beef. What is it called?"

Nhual translated, and he and his wife started laughing heartily. The American, however, started to squirm nervously.

"Oh, no," he said. "What did I just eat, Nhual?"

Again Nhual and his wife guffawed as Don's face reddened.

Nhual said, "We call it *rok*, Trung-uy!"

Concerned, Bendell said, "What's *rok* mean?"

"Maybe I better not tell." Nhual chuckled, "Maybe you get sick."

"Oh, shit! C'mon, Nhual," Bendell said while Nhual, still laughing, translated.

"Cow!" Nhual roared amid fits of laughter.

Shortly, even Plar had awakened, and they all laughed uproariously.

Bendell pulled out two cigarillos, stuck one in Nhual's mouth, one in his own, and lit both.

"I gotta go home," he said. "I go up on the mountain tomorrow."

Nhual pointed to a tunnel entrance by the door. "That

tunnel goes right to your bunker. You will be with Harry Boyle, Trung-uy. The Jeh like him. Always friendly, always happy. He is commo man, Commo Willy's boss."

"That tunnel goes to my bunker?"

"Yeah, Americans built tunnels between all bunkers, TOC, and team house," the little man replied. "How you like bracelet?"

Don Bendell looked down at the hand-engraved brass bracelet on his left wrist.

"I love it," he said, "Why did the village chief give it to me?"

"He says you are close friend," Nhual replied deftly, slipping a second bracelet on Bendell's wrist. Smiling, he said "Now you have two."

Hands in his pockets, Bendell smiled warmly. His hand flashed and there was a click, swish, and lock sound. Nhual looked down at the switchblade knife sticking into the board at his side. It had a red coral handle inlaid with gold dragons.

"For you, my friend," Bendell said. " 'Night, Nhual."

"Trung-uy, call me Ba Nua, please."

"Okay," Bendell replied, "What's that mean?"

Pointing to his daughter, he said, "It means 'father of Nua.' My closest friends call me that."

The two shook hands, Bendell imitating the Jeh custom of shaking with the right hand while holding your right wrist with the left hand.

"G'night, Trung-uy. I'll take Plar to her bunker," Ba Nua said. "Tell Harry Boyle I say he's a cowboy."

" 'Night. Thank you."

Making his way down the narrow tunnel, Bendell thought back to the tunnel at Camp A.P. Hill, Virginia. He started to develop a slight claustrophobic panic but fought it back quickly. The tunnel ran under the driveway for a good thirty feet. It was hand dug out and shored up with small boards, but there were occasional spots with small cave-ins. A single light bulb illuminated it. It came out right next to the team's heart, the Tactical Operations Center, which held all the intelligence maps and papers, Harry Boyle and Commo Willy's bunkers, and their commo room with its big single sideband radio. To the left of the tunnel egress, five dirt steps went up into a concrete 4.2-inch mortar bunker, recessed four feet into the ground. Bendell walked up these steps and across the pit. To his right, five more steps went down into a big ammo bunker, and straight ahead, directly below a concrete and sandbagged .50-caliber machine-gun emplacement, five more dirt steps went down to the plywood door that opened into Bendell and Joe Howard's tiny bunker. A plywood wall ran the length of the dirt-walled twelve-by-twelve underground structure. There were two tiny, funnel-shaped shooting ports which also served as windows. Nailed under each shooting port, as in the other Americans' bunkers, were several electronic detonators and a wooden sketch. The sketch would show the part of the camp's perimeter in front of the shooting port, and the location of hidden claymore mines that would blast thousands of deadly steel pellets outward like a giant shotgun blast. Also hidden and sketched were buried fifty-five-gallon drums of fugas, with explosive charges underneath. By mixing soap and several chemicals in fifty-five-gallon drums of Air Force jet fuel, a deadly napalmlike substance had been created and hidden for further protection in case of a full-scale attack.

Don knew that Joe would not be in the bunker, as it was his turn on radio watch in the team house for the first half of the night.

He started down the steps to his bunker as he heard a tiny, almost imperceptible, noise in his darkened room. He had acquired a Smith and Wesson .357 Magnum and quick-draw holster on the black market in Nha Trang before coming to camp. Everybody wore a handgun around camp, but normally carried rifles out in the jungle or while traveling. The gun was quickly in his hand, his other hand on the door handle.

With a lunge he opened the door with his left hand and flipped on the switch, diving into the bunker headfirst, as his right hand cocked and pointed the revolver at the figure before him. He landed at Ning's feet and looked up at her grinning, beautiful face. From the floor he could look into her eyes and see her gorgeous breasts at the same time. They both froze, except for the smiles breaking out on their faces.

Grinning devilishly, she said, "You tell me I see you later. You right."

She unhooked her *atok*, and the black silk skirt fell around her bare feet. All that Ning wore was a big smile and one strand of beaded string, which hung down around her waist and dipped low just above her sparse triangle of pubic hair. Bendell heard that the Yards had very little body hair and now saw that it was true.

Heart pounding in his throat, he rose slowly. One of the first things Don had learned was that nobody wore underwear beneath their jungle fatigues in 'Nam because of the unbearable humidity and heat. This fact now proved to be embarrassing, as his erection bulged outward in his pants. Easily noticing this, Ning started giggling.

"You glad see me," she said, teasing.

Embarrassed, Bendell said, "Ning, I . . . ah . . . you should go."

Seductively she said, "Trung-uy no make me go," then, grinning, "You make me come."

Flushed and flustered, Don said, "Ning, why are you here?"

"War, Trung-uy," she said. "Me think fast. You love Montagnard *beaucoup*. I see. Me want you."

Their faces were inches apart, and Bendell thought he would have a heart attack. He also felt like his balls were going to explode like an HE round.

"Ning," he said with a sigh, "I can't deal with this. I have a wife."

She replaced her skirt, but the two kept staring into each other's eyes.

Smiling softly, Ning said, "This is different world. One hour, maybe I die. Maybe you die." She paused and touched his face. "Me know me love you *beaucoup*. Soon you love Ning same-same. Good night, Trung-uy."

Standing on her tiptoes, the very tall Jeh beauty put her arms around his neck and gave the American a very long, lingering, passionate kiss. She left.

Bendell sat down on his bunk, then stood, then sat and uttered a long sigh. Might as well do something useful.

He grabbed a BAR, his browning automatic rifle, belt and harness, and a handful of loaded twenty-round magazines for his CAR-15. He put three magazines upside down in each ammo pouch and then fit one magazine on top under the ammo-pouch flap. At that time M16 and CAR-15 magazines were noted for having weak springs, so he only put eighteen instead of twenty rounds in each magazine. Another trick he had learned from his NCO watch guards at Bragg was to make the thirteenth, sixteenth, seventeenth, and eighteenth rounds all tracers. That way, when in the heat of battle, he would know when a magazine was really about to run out. He would carry them upside down to keep out dirt and rain and grab them and load them more easily. He also had learned to eject the empty magazine and toss it down the front of his shirt.

Don had also taped a K-bar knife and sheath upside down on the harness webbing. He had attached two high-explosive hand grenades, several smoke grenades, a first-aid pouch, two canteens, and a can containing serum albumin, a blood expander, in an IV bottle.

"Bark! Bark! Bark!" Gypsy, Bendell's German shepherd, was chasing a rabbit across his backyard in Fayetteville, North Carolina. "Bark! Bark!"

He opened his eyes and looked at the logs and mud,

one foot above his head. Bark! Bark! He could not figure out where that barking was coming from. He emerged from a crude bunker and saw Harry Boyle drinking coffee by the fire. Don relieved his bladder and looked around for the dog.

"Hey, Sergeant Boyle!" he yelled. "Where the hell is the dog that's barking?"

Harry laughed, "Not a dog, sir. That's a barking deer, down there in the jungle. About the size of a medium dog."

"No shit?" Bendell yelled, still urinating.

"No shit!" he yelled. "Jungle's full of 'em!"

The redheaded sergeant looked at the lieutenant as he approached. Dressed in a "tiger suit," a camouflage uniform, Bendell had a week's growth of beard, a camo cowboy hat, and a black scarf around his neck. He wore his .347 Magnum in the quick-draw holster. He also was wearing an Army camo poncho liner with a neckhole cut in it.

"Clint Eastwood!" Harry yelled,

With a mock leer Bendell flipped his poncho liner up over his shoulder. Clamping down on the cigar with his teeth, he spit, but the saliva bounced off the cigar and dropped on his boot.

Harry Boyle hit his leg and fell backward off his log, laughing hysterically.

Bendell looked at the spit on his muddy jungle boot and said, "Shit!"

Harry rolled on the ground laughing. Finally recovering, he sat up, poured Bendell a cup of coffee, and handed it to him.

"Trung-uy Bendell," he said, "you ain't gonna hear the end of this!"

Laughing, Don said, "Harry Boyle, if you tell a soul . . ."

Harry replied, "Sir, everybody worth a shit in SF has a nickname. Now you do too."

"Oh, you redheaded rat fucker," Bendell responded.

Laughing, Harry said, "At least I don't eat the damn things."

"Hey, I'm gonna eat what the Yards eat."

"Good," Harry said, and chuckled. "I sure hope none of 'em are queer."

"Oh, fuck you!" Bendell responded to the laughing NCO.

Harry stood up. "I gotta go back to my radios. Commo Willy relieves me today. I'm going on R and R in less than two months, did I tell you?" he said with enthusiasm.

He reached in his pants pocket, pulled out a picture of a devastatingly beautiful Latin lady, and showed it to Bendell.

"My wife," he said, just glowing. "Meeting her in Hawaii! I show you her picture?"

"About a hundred times, Harry Boyle." Bendell laughed. "She really is beautiful."

"I know," Harry replied, looking longingly at her picture. "She's living near L.A. and doesn't speak a word of English. I just can't get killed, Lieutenant."

"Shit, you're SF," Bendell said, "You won't!"

Harry smiled and turned, then paused momentarily and walked on. A shiver ran up and down Bendell's spine.

During the following week Bendell had his first exposure to the Army of Ho Chi Minh. The mountaintop his company occupied had twin peaks, separated by a deep, jungle-choked chasm. It was unoccupied, or so he thought. Actually a company of North Vietnamese had moved in and set up a perimeter, digging deep foxholes with little bunkers at the bottom, that had just enough room for one man to sit in. While Commo Willy was unloading supplies off a Huey helicopter and Bendell was talking on the AN-PRC-25, or Prick 25, radio, the NVA started lobbing 82-mm mortars onto their position.

The Huey took off immediately, and Commo Willy literally did a headfirst somersault as it did so and landed, running to the 81-mm mortar. Without a sight he started firing mortars back at the NVA. In the meantime Bendell started calling in and adjusting indirect fire from a 4.2-inch mortar and a 155 Howitzer battery at Dak Pek; a Fourth Division 105 Howitzer battery which was two FSBs to the south; and a Fourth Division 4.2-inch mortar from the next FSB to the south.

Afterward he was quite pleased with himself, and thankful for all his OCS training on adjusting indirect firepower. Unfortunately, even after having tons of ordnance pound in on their position, the gutsy NVA started lobbing more mortar rounds in on the Dak Pek force.

An Air Force forward air controller flew in from Dak To, and Bendell directed the FAC onto the enemy target. He brought in some F-4 jets, which dropped five hundred pound bombs, 20-mm cannon, CBUs, or cluster bomb units, and napalm on the enemy target.

Next he brought in two pairs of American-trained Vietnamese pilots in prop-driven AIE Skyraiders, who also dropped more ordnance. The subsequent bomb damage assessment patrol found the foxhole bunkers with the personnel dead inside, lungs collapsed from the oxygen-sucking napalm having detonated. Four wounded NVA soldiers were there when the patrol arrived but quickly took off.

One night during the week Bendell listened on the radio as a Fourth Division ambush patrol called in that someone was moving near their claymore mines. He said he was going to blow his claymores, and Bendell, remembering lessons from his NCOs at Bragg, wanted to scream *"No!"* into the radio. Too late, he heard a couple of claymores detonate in the distance and knew what had happened. A few minutes later another voice called in a spot report listing two Americans as KIA, killed in action. An NVA had simply snuck in and turned the claymores around, facing the GIs. He then withdrew and tossed pebbles and sticks to make noise until they set off the antipersonnel mines in their own faces.

On another night he and Commo Willy listened as two Fourth Division soldiers spoke to two others in a listening post, whom they were going to relieve. On the way they found a trip wire attached to a CBU booby trap. They warned the two in the LP about it and said they would guide them back to the company perimeter. Not long afterward Bendell and Williams heard the booby trap go off and learned that one was killed and that another had to be medevaced.

Commo Willy told Bendell about a 101st Airborne Division LRRP patrol operating out of Dak Pek before the Fourth Division had arrived. The patrol found a 4.2-inch, undetonated HE mortar round lodged in the fork of a small tree. One of the patrol members shook it out and wiped out all but one man on the team. Another time Chuck Challela, Dak Pek's light-weapons NCO, had been leading a company of Yards on a joint operation with a company from the 101st. Before going out, Chuck had pointed out an old French mine field to the 101st company commander. Chuck warned the captain to keep his men away from the mine field. Two days later four Americans were killed, and ten severely wounded, trying to cross the mine field. The two talked about how many Americans got killed out of their own or some commander's sheer stupidity or lack of common sense. They agreed the figure had to be way above fifty percent, and they thanked God for watching over Special Forces.

They both knew that there were idiots in SF also, but they took comfort in knowing there were also some of the best soldiers in the world, who had enough balls to countermand, or get around, an order that would needlessly get a soldier killed. SF has always taken care of its own, while most military units traditionally ate their young.

Two weeks after Harry went back to Dak Pek in anticipation of his upcoming R and R, Bendell and Commo Willy came down off the mountain more experienced, much wiser, and much, much older.

In Vietnam, good SF men traveled as light as possible. This meant the clothes they were wearing, a jungle sweater, ammo, food, water, medical supplies, weapons, a poncho, and a nylon jungle hammock. A razor, soap, and things of that nature were frivolities. They didn't wear helmets or flak jackets or any of the heavy equipment conventional units had to wear and carry, preferring instead to travel light and be much more mobile. Bendell was now sporting a three-week growth of beard, crud, and bamboo nicks and scratches, all of which needed to be drowned and lathered and re-drowned.

The first person he ran into was Plar, who ran up and gave him a big hug and kiss.

"*Chung-wi ba Plar,*" she squealed, "*Mi liem jei!*"

"*Trung-uy lo ayou Plar!*" he replied.

Excited, Plar blurted, "Trung-wi speak Jeh!"

Smiling, Bendell said, "Yes, Suat started teaching me."

Nhual walked up as Don set Plar down and shook hands.

Hey, Trung-uy," he said, grinning, "first operation and you kick ass, huh?"

"Oh, hell . . ."

Nhual went on. "In three weeks we have big camp celebration. Some Fourth Division officers come. Jeh warriors dance, play gong, drink *beaucoup* rice wine . . . you'll like it."

"*Hey liem jei, Ba Nua!*" Bendell said enthusiastically.

Grinning, Nhual said, "You learn Jeh, huh? Good. Many village chiefs and strikers want you to visit and *hut nhiaa.*"

"*Hut nhiaa?*"

"Yeah," Nhual said. "Drink rice wine."

Ba Nua smiled as he looked beyond Don, who now turned to see a broadly smiling Ning walk up to him and give him a long, lingering, passionate kiss while Plar giggled.

She stepped back. "Hello, Nhual. Hello, Plar. Trung-uy, you miss Ning?"

Husky-voiced, the tall, bearded soldier said, "Yes, yes, I did."

Smiling seductively, she grabbed his hand and led him to his bunker. Grinning, Nhual watched them walk away and then led Plar by the hand.

"Nhual, where Daddy me go?" the little girl inquired.

Nhual chuckled. "Little one, your daddy went to explore the underground tunnels. You will see him later."

... 11 ...

ANOTHER NARROW ESCAPE

There was a low rumbling noise in the distance. A daily
occurrence in the Central Highlands, it sounded like the
muffled noise of pins scattering in a far-off bowling alley.
It was an arc light, a B-52 strike.

Kok carefully turned the squelch knob on the radio in
front of him. Headphones on, he couldn't hear the distant
B-52 strike in the cramped radio room, but he did sense
the presence of someone approaching.

Indeed somebody, a Montagnard, was just now passing
the sign on the front lawn that read: USAID—UNITED STATES
AGENCY FOR INTERNATIONAL DEVELOPMENT, QUAN DUC,
REPUBLIC OF SOUTH VIETNAM. He ran into the radio room
breathless, and Kok, puzzled, removed the headphones.

"What's wrong?" Kok asked.

"Kok, the—" he began, but Kok hunched his shoulders
and held his finger up to his mouth in a shushing gesture.
The wiry Dega looked around for potential eavesdroppers
as the other Montagnard, aware of his mistake, started
again, a sheepish expression on his face.

"Siu Ton," he said, correcting himself, "the Vietnamese found out that you're here. They are hiding outside
your apartment. You must leave right away."

"I will have to find a way to Ban Me Thuot," Kok said
thoughtfully.

"No," the Dega replied. "Y Bham wants you to go to Nha Trang."

"Nha Trang, that's on the coast." Kok gasped. "Why there?"

The man continued. "Y Bham wants you to get a job and then start recruiting and training Dega for FULRO in the Mike Force. There are many good Dega there."

"Okay, but first I must go to Ban Me Thout and find out more about my mission," Kok said. "Besides, I made friends with a Vietnamese police captain while I've been here and got him to give me more ID papers with my false name."

"Okay," the man replied. "Just don't go to your apartment."

A few minutes later Kok stood outside his boss's office, rubbing his eyes until they watered. He entered, and his boss, an American, got a concerned look on his face.

"What's wrong, Siu Ton?" he said.

"Mr. Gaspard, I have emergency. I must go to Ban Me Thuot right now," Kok said between fake sobs.

"Sure," the sympathetic American civilian responded. "But it's almost dark; why not wait until morning?"

Kok put his head in his hands and faked more tears.

"Mr. Gaspard, my grandfather is dying. If I wait, he will be dead by tomorrow. I must go. Please?"

"Okay, Siu Ton," Mr. Gaspard said, "I'm really sorry about your grandfather. Call yourself a plane in to take you to Ban Me Thuot."

Kok jumped up, smiling. "Thanks, boss! Thank you. I will be back soon!"

Kok hated lying, and he liked George Gaspard very much, but he also knew his life was at stake. He called in a plane and walked to the runway so he would not arouse suspicion.

Two days later, in Ban Me Thuot, a FULRO warrior awakened Kok with a grin. "Kok, we just got word from

Quan Duc. Yesterday the Yuan MPs went into your apartment, shot holes in your bed, and tore up everything, like a tiger tears out a pig's entrails.''

Kok lay there, and a laugh started rumbling deep within his belly.

... 12 ...

YARDS

Bendell's mind kept jumping from his childhood to the present as he watched the Jeh dancers in front of him. Wearing black loincloths and a jungle of beaded bracelets, necklaces, and earrings, the warriors danced around the sacrificial cows on the parade ground. Like the rest of the American SF team members, Bendell was seated in the second row of metal folding chairs, behind the LLDB team. The young lieutenant had started American Indian fancy dancing at the age of five. Watching these warriors slowly dancing, spears and knives in hand, to the beat of several brass gongs and wooden drums, he thought back to his childhood. He pictured himself showing off during the village dance, wearing a horsehair roach headdress, and colorful, plumed Oklahoma U-bustles on the back of his neck, at the small of his back, and on each arm and leg. He realized then why he loved the Dega so; they reminded him of the American Indians of the 1800s.

To Don's left sat Nhual, and to his right sat several officers from the First Brigade, Fourth Infantry Division headquarters at Dak To. Four giant, colorful, fringed, and decorated bamboo poles stood in front of the onlookers. Between each sat a giant crock of fermented Montagnard rice wine. A sacrificial cow was tethered to each decorated pole, and it was around these that the warriors now danced.

To the cheers of the onlookers, at a simultaneous silent signal, four dancers thrust long bamboo steel-tipped spears through the left side of each cow, the tips thrusting out the other side. Others captured the blood spurting out and poured it on the crocks of rice wine. The throng now gathered around the dying cows as the beasts were quickly butchered and divided, and the parts passed out. The Jeh ate everything from the cow, even the hide; nothing was left of the four cows in five minutes' time.

Vietnamese and Americans gathered around the crocks of rice wine to drink "sticks." The Dega fermented rice, water, rat tails, potatoes, and other ingredients in a smooth-tasting but potent brew. They put a hollow reed in the center of the large earthen crock, then placed a piece of rubber hose on the end of the reed. A bamboo stick rested across the top of the jar, with another four-inch long stick extending downward into the brew. Each drinker who was passed the hose had to drink the liquid down to the level below the four-inch stick without removing the hose from his lips. If not, the crock was again filled to the top, and he would have to try again. The rice swelled continuously, raising the level of the wine, so the longer he took to get the level down, the more he had to drink.

Lieutenant Bendell had been invited to drink sticks with almost every Montagnard in camp that day, it seemed, and he was quite drunk by mid-afternoon. Nhual, who accompanied him, pretended to drink but never touched a drop the whole day. Don was enjoying a drinking contest with Mr. Lon, a Cambodian who was commander of Alpha Company. Seated in Mr. Lon's bunker, Bendell had been eating pieces of boiled cow lung, which he drunkenly referred to as sponges, and drank moonshine whiskey with American beer for chasers. He was too drunk even to be concerned when he learned that the still for the rotgut had been constructed with the lead-lined radiator from an Army deuce-and-a-half. Nhual took Bendell's arm as he led him from Mr. Lon's bunker. Don laughed loudly as they walked across Alpha Company's hilltop, but Nhual was quiet and serious.

Nhual whispered, "Trung-uy, have you noticed the two Vietnamese who have been following us today? Don't look!"

Sobering, Lieutenant Bendell said, "Yeah, what about 'em?"

"They are . . . oh, shit . . . what do you call them?"

"Spies?" Don asked.

"No," Nhual replied. "Uh . . . hit men!" That's it, hit men! The Vietnamese hired them to kill you!"

Shocked, Bendell said, "Kill me! Why? Well, fuck," he said, starting to turn, but Nhual stopped him. "Let's just turn around and shoot the little peckerheads!"

Holding Don's arm, Nhual scooted him along. "No! No, don't worry. You are protected. Don't worry. C'mon, one more bunker. His name is Bayh, and he's the head of the recon platoon."

"Why do they wanna dust me?" Bendell asked, slurring.

"I will explain at Bayh's bunker. Those two will disappear as soon as it is dark," Nhual answered.

"Disappear?" Bendell said.

The sun had been up for two hours when Nhual ran down the steps into Don's bunker and knocked on the door.

"*Trung-uy!* Get up!" he yelled.

A minute later, wearing a towel and a six-shooter, Bendell walked with Nhual toward the shower room.

"Ba Nua, was Bayh serious last night?"

"Very serious," Nhual responded. "But, listen, you must hurry. A squad of NVA ambushed some villagers this morning at Dak Wen Tung. Several were wounded, Bac-Si is too busy to go out there, and you know villagers: They don't come to dispensary."

They arrived at the door of the shower room and walked in. Don said, "Okay, I'll hurry. Will you have somebody bring me a cup of coffee and a can of Pepsi?"

"Me bring," Ning said from the doorway, her big grin widening. "You already drink *beaucoup* today."

Bendell, smiling, took the steaming cup and the pop and took a swig of each. "I didn't drink, Ning. A tiger ate me and shit me over a cliff."

An hour later Lieutenant Bendell, Nhual, and six strikers who stood around Bendell like secret servicemen were in the center of Dak Wen Tung. Don did not know it then, but as of the previous evening, the six silent shadows would always be nearby as bodyguards. If Bendell were killed, each of them would die first; if not, the survivors would die painful deaths at the hands of their own people.

Hundreds of miles away at FULRO headquarters, Y Bham Enoul was having orders drawn up, appointing Bendell as a brigadier general in the FULRO, responsible for thirty thousand Jeh and some Sedang and Halong. Bendell never would publicly confirm or deny whether he had accepted the appointment.

Drenched with sweat, Bendell sat on the edge of a woven bamboo *marao*, drinking from his canteen. "Damn," he said, "it's hotter than a flamethrower's dick. Must be a hundred and twenty degrees and one hundred percent humidity."

Nhual said quietly, "She was shot through her ass by AK-47." Several villagers were carrying a moaning, wrinkled old woman forward.

They laid her facedown on the *marao* as curious villagers watched. Bendell pulled her waistband from her *atok* and peeked at her wounded buttocks.

Grinning, he covered her butt and smiled at the villagers. *"Oh liem jei! Liem Jei!"*

While all the villagers laughed, the old lady, blushing and giggling, slapped his arm with an oh-you gesture.

Asking her to go to the dispensary, Don said, *"Y dra-dra, au wa mi chiu nhia pogang?"*

"Dei!" she replied, sharply saying she wouldn't go and telling him to go. *"Au dei wa chiu! Lih Tonang, mi chiu,"* she finished with a gesture meant to wave him off.

Bendell asked, *"Y dra-dra?"*

But she shooed him away, so he walked off, frustrated, and lit a cigarette while Nhual spoke to her quietly. He walked back over to Don.

"What'd she say, Ba Nua?"

"She say you can smile and call her grandmother all day," he answered, "but she still won't go to no damn dispensary."

"Sa ai?" Bendell yelled to the woman.

She motioned Nhual over and spoke again.

Turning to Don, he said, "She says that evil spirits lurk in the dispensary and will kill her and hide her spirit in the jungle."

Bendell took off his beret and rubbed his short hair as he paced. "Ask her if I lie."

Nhual translated, and she looked at Bendell, shaking her head no. She spoke emphatically. *"Dei! Dei kal ai?"*

Bendell said calmly, "Now ask her if she trusts me."

Nhual translated, and she shook her head affirmatively, saying, *"A-dei."*

Pausing, Don then said, "Now ask her if she'll go if I carry her myself and leave a guard with her all day and all night."

Nhual translated, and she set her jaw, saying emphatically, *"Dei!"*

Pacing again, Bendell said, "Shit, Ba Nua, tell her that if she doesn't go, her ass is gonna rot and fall off!"

Nhual again translated the commando's words, and the woman got a very frightened look on her leathery face. She motioned the officer over and he complied.

"Lih tonang, au chiu," she said resignedly.

Don smiled as several villagers, amid cheers, picked

her up and placed her on the American's back. With Nhual, the bodyguards, and his moaning burden, he left the village, dreading the long journey to the dispensary.

The jungle trees had all been cut away around the village and the camp proper, but this was a tropical climate and resurgent undergrowth and tanglefoot was a monumental obstacle throughout the valley. Bendell's uniform was soaked with sweat in minutes, as if he had just fallen into the ocean. Demons flew in his mouth with each breath and tried to tear his lungs out and pull them out into that hot, wet blast furnace.

The closer he got to the Dak Poko River, the worse the undergrowth got, but he finally made it. Almost incoherent with the exertion, Bendell fell twice into the cold, clear river, but the icy mountain waters revived him. His legs felt as if he were trying to walk through quicksand wearing concrete-filled hip-waders. In OCS his tac officer had made his platoon low-crawl through Raider Creek for hours, and he had had to do thousands of push-ups, but he couldn't remember being this tired, this muscle and bone-weary.

His SF ego kept him going; he had given his word. The dispensary, now out of focus in Bendell's normal twenty-ten vision, wavered in front of him. He knew each staggering step took him that much closer, but his mind wandered to other things. His legs bent almost to a squatting position, he made it through the door of the dispensary and lay the woman on the cot. Bendell fainted and fell across the next cot, the blond American medic watching on in wonder. Then the medic looked at Nhual for an explanation as he began checking Bendell's vital signs.

"Bac-Si, he carry woman far," Nhual explained. "NVA shoot her through her ass."

"Why did you let him, Nhual?" the medic raged. "He's got heat exhaustion! Bring me some salt pills and water," he said, indicating where Nhual could find them.

... 13 ...

NHA TRANG

Kok held the attention of the roomful of Dega, all members of the Fifth Special Forces Group, Mike Force. Airborne-qualified strikers, these were the best of the best and were shuffled all over Vietnam to reinforce A-camps or B- or C-Team Mike Forces under attack by enemy forces. Many of these men were Rhade from the Ban Me Thuot area and were already members of the FULRO movement.

Kok said, "The communists spoke to Y Bham under a flag of truce. They said they just wanted the Dega to back off and not fight, and when they win the war, we can have the Central Highlands back as our country."

One Dega said, "And what did Y Bham say to them?"

Kok grinned. "What would you say? Can we trust the Yuan from the north any more than the Yuan from the south? He told them that the Americans are our friends and all Yuan are our enemies."

A number of strikers in the room nodded their heads in affirmative compliance.

Kok continued. "The Americans promised to give us back our autonomy. They are the only ones who do not lie to us. If we turn our backs on our friends, then we are no better than the Vietnamese."

Just then a jeep passed by the building. In it was Don Bendell, with Plar riding on his lap. In her hand was a rag doll and in his a weapon. A few minutes later the jeep passed through a gate with several MP sentries and a sign that read: HEADQUARTERS, FIFTH SPECIAL FORCES GROUP (AIRBORNE)—FIRST SPECIAL FORCES, NHA TRANG, REPUBLIC OF VIETNAM.

Plar was dressed in a cute dress, part of a clothing offering to his camp from an American church. Don was very tan and now wore ten Yard bracelets on each wrist, and two beaded necklaces.

Grinning at Plar, he said, "Plar, you want to try an American ice-cream cone?"

Her eyes lit up with excitement, "Number-one thou!"

The next morning, with Plar napping in his room, Lieutenant Bendell jumped to attention as the Fifth Group commander, Colonel Aaron, entered the group briefing room. With Bendell were two sergeants from two other Special Forces camps in the Central Highlands. Outside the door stood two spit-and-polish MPs at parade rest, and a small tripod with a sign that read: GROUP COMMANDER'S BRIEFING CLASSIFIED, and below, in red letters, the word SECRET.

Colonel Aaron, a distinguished-looking full bird colonel, said, "As you were, gentlemen. Smoke if you got 'em."

The three commandos sat down and lit cigarettes. The two jangled, like Bendell, every time their arms moved, due to all the brass bracelets.

The CO looked at the three SF troopers, a pleasant smile on his face, and started speaking. "I will remind you, gentlemen, that this briefing is classified as secret and is not to be discussed outside of this room. It will be automatically downgraded at four-year intervals and declassified at the end of twelve years."

You were summoned here to discuss the FULRO movement.''

The three eyed each other, near grins appearing on each man's face.

The CO continued. ''I am not going to give you three an explanation of the FULRO movement. Recent intelligence reports indicated that you three either have been offered leadership positions in FULRO or may be offered such a position in the near future.''

Bendell studied the burning end of his Lucky Strike as the commander went on. ''As you three realize, it is one of the goals of the FULRO movement to overthrow the South Vietnamese government in Saigon. Virtually every Special Forces man who is now or has served with the Yards loves and respects them very much. You three are all in CA/PO positions on your respective A-teams, which probably put you in an even closer relationship with the indigenous people.

''We all sympathize with the plight of the Montagnards, but I want to remind you three of our official position. The South Vietnamese are our allies, and any of our people who are caught working with, or for, the FULRO will be court-martialed and could, if convicted, be looking at a thirty-year stretch in Leavenworth.''

The three men looked at each other, still suppressing grins, then back at Colonel Aaron, who wore a friendly smile.

He asked, ''Are there any questions, gentlemen? If not, this briefing is concluded and you may return to your A-detachments.''

He got up and the three snapped to attention as he walked past them and out of the over-polished briefing room. As soon as the door closed, all three started laughing and shook hands firmly.

One of the sergeants, grinning broadly, spoke to Bendell with a Southern accent. ''Loo-tenant, ah shore don't wanna do nothin' that would piss off our loyal allies . . . the LLVC. Do you, sir?"

Laughing, Bendell slapped him on the back and replied, "Fuck, no, Sergeant. We ought to buy every one of 'em a blow job from Sweet Lips in Pleiku."

Laughing, the other sergeant said, "You know Sweet Lips, Trung-uy?"

Bendell laughed. "No, but I heard she gives the best head jobs in 'Nam."

"Fuckin' A, Tweety Bird," he responded enthusiastically. "You get within a mile of her mouth, you'll pop yer nuts."

Leaving the briefing room, Bendell went to the Group commo bunker to read the Teletype and to get the latest news. He got the latest news blurb about Bobby Kennedy's recent assassination and then saw a brief report about some KIAs at Dak Pek.

He ran over to a commo sergeant seated at a sideband radio console.

Very concerned, Don said, "Sergeant, what the hell happened at Dak Pek . . . A-242?"

The sergeant looked up. "Your camp, sir?"

Bendell nodded and the commo specialist went on. "Well, the scoop I got, sir, is that a bunch of your team members were firing a 60-mm mortar, and a round was booby-trapped and exploded coming out of tube."

"Oh, fuck me," Bendell exclaimed in shock and disbelief. "Who got hurt?"

"Well, let's see," the operator recalled. "Several got medevaced and two were killed, some guy visiting your camp and your senior radio operator."

Bendell sat down, mouth open, "Harry Boyle. He was leaving on R and R today." He stood, thanked the NCO, and left.

An hour later Plar and Bendell were seated alone on an HUID helicopter as it lifted off a Nha Trang helipad. The young lieutenant pulled his beret off his head and buried his face in it. Plar looked up, at first puzzled, and then put her little arms around his neck.

It was nighttime in Dak Pek. Ning lay asleep on Bendell's bunk as he walked up to the .50-caliber machine gun above his bunker and found the team engineer–demolitions specialist, Sergeant Larry Crotsley, looking up at the starlit sky.

"Beer, sir?" Larry offered, taking a swig himself.

"Thanks," Bendell replied as he opened it, looking up at the starry sky.

"I was just thinking . . ." Larry said.

"What's that?" queried Bendell.

"I can't believe I was the one who fired that mortar," Larry said. "It exploded just as it left the tube and I wasn't even touched. All those others were killed and wounded," he continued, obviously puzzled.

Bendell pulled out a cigarette and started to light it. There were six rapid flashes from inside Alpha Company's perimeter, and Bendell's beret was snatched off his head as six cracks were heard over the men's heads. This was followed by the actual reports of the automatic weapon, which were six staccato *whump* sounds. By this time Larry and Don were both flat on the concrete floor of the machine-gun bunker, their knees bruised. They didn't remain there, however. Crotsley grabbed the machine gun, violently jerking the cocking handle back twice. Bendell grabbed and opened a metal tube that contained a pyrotechnic device, a hand-held parachute flare that someone had cached with the others in the bottom of the big machine-gun bunker.

Crotsley said, "Shit, that came from within the camp!"

"Yeah, from Alpha Company! Ready?" the lieutenant replied.

"Fire away, Clint!" Larry yelled, then corrected himself. "I mean, Lieutenant."

Bendell grinned as he turned and fired the hand-held flare over Alpha Company's hill. Larry jumped up, both thumbs on the twin rear triggers of the big machine gun, ready to open fire. Unfortunately, by this time many people had come out of their bunkers to find out what the firing was about. Several Americans ran out of the team house, weapons in hand. One NCO had a shotgun in one hand and a poker hand in the other.

Mike, now wearing railroad tracks (captain's bars), shouted, "What's happening?"

"A fuckin' sniper at Alpha Company just put six rounds over our heads with an automatic weapon!" Bendell yelled. "M16, I think!"

"See 'em?" Mike yelled.

"No, sir!" Bendell replied.

After looking and milling around, everybody seemed to return to their business. Jumping down to the steps of his bunker, Don looked back up at the large NCO.

"Sergeant Crotsley, you get your answer about the mortar?"

"What?" Larry asked.

Grinning, Bendell looked up at the many stars in the night sky. Larry looked up, then started grinning. The two men looked at each other and smiled, then the officer disappeared into his bunker.

Ning was awake, but her eyes were very puffy.

"Yuan, they say you leader here FULRO," she said. "Try kill you again and again, same-same."

"I know." He sighed resignedly.

Ning's eyes clouded with tears and she started crying. Bendell grabbed her arms, alarmed.

Choked up, she was sobbing. "They kill ones you love same-same."

"What?" he replied in shock, then, looking around, "Ning, where's Plar? Where is Plar!"

The raven-haired beauty burst out with racking sobs and threw herself against his chest. He held her tightly and looked around the room, eyes darting everywhere with stress and worry.

"Oh, God, no!" he said, choking up, realization hitting him.

He looked at the adoption papers sitting on his foot-locker, and his eyes filled with tears.

... 14 ...

ANOTHER NAIL BITER

The bay in Nha Trang bounced sparkles of reflected sunlight as Kok left work for the day. He waved good night to several Americans and Vietnamese employees. A bee buzzed by his ear and flew past the sign he had passed, which read, PACIFIC ARCHITECT AND ENGINEERING.

Besides recruiting and training FULRO at Nha Trang's Mike Force, he had done well at PA&E, as an administrative assistant, still under the alias of Siu Ton.

As Kok walked toward the apartment he shared with five Filipinos, a Montagnard walked up beside him and Kok nodded.

"Kok, you are in danger," he said. "I checked on your secretary, like you asked."

Kok stopped and looked at him. "Yes?" Kok asked.

The man went on. "Her brother is the chief of military security for Nha Trang."

"Okay, thank you," Kok said. "God has given me the feeling again that I am in danger."

Kok walked on, carefully approaching his apartment. He spotted several Vietnamese police jeeps and a few men watching his apartment. Quickly he withdrew and made his way back to PA&E. He found one of his roommates, the head of security for PA&E, and convinced him to take him to Mike Force headquarters.

Two hours later, carrying phony leave papers, two M16 rifles, and wearing strike-force boots, uniform, and hat, Kok was driven by his apartment in a U.S. Army three-quarter-ton truck.

QCs were everywhere, and he saw his Filipino roommates being questioned by angry Vietnamese military authorities.

On the plane an hour later, Kok closed his eyes and said a prayer of thanks. He opened his eyes and smiled.

Next to him, a haughty Vietnamese, also on his way to Ban Me Thuot, said, "What are you grinning at?"

Kok smiled now. "I was just thinking of how much clothes and luggage I have donated to your government."

The Vietnamese screwed his face up with a questioning look, shrugged his shoulders, and turned his back to the now chuckling Montagnard.

... 15 ...

MORE HITS

Bendell, driving a Dak Pek jeep down the driveway, slid
to a stop next to Suat, the interpreter, who was walking
down to the river.

"Hey, where you cowboys going?" the fifteen-year-old
father of two asked, looking at the jeep full of Montagnards with Bendell.

The stocky young Jeh had been hired by the A-team as
an interpreter at the age of twelve, after having killed a
Vietnamese man in a fight with his bare hands.

As Bendell reached into a bag next to him and pulled
out a hand grenade, Nhual explained. "Trung-uy's taking
us fishing!"

Excited, Suat jumped in and the jeep took off. Turning
south, Bendell skirted the runway and finally parked at the
suspension bridge strung across the Dak Pek River, near
its intersection with the wide, swirling Dak Poko.

He and the strikers grabbed their weapons and headed
west along the Dak Pek. Finding a quiet pool along the
rushing river, the strikers, joined by others who had
walked, soon stripped off their clothing and lined up along
the riverbank, eyes riveted on the American lieutenant and
his bag. Others, still clothed, stood guard along the bank.

"Ready?" Bendell asked as Nhual nodded positively.

The officer pulled a grenade from the bag, pulled the

pin, and tossed it into the water. In seconds the muffled explosion emerged as giant bubbles. The Jeh dived in and started surfacing with stunned, carplike fish clutched in their teeth and hands. Tossing them on shore, they dived down for more.

Don threw a number of grenades in the water and watched the industrious fish harvesters. He thought back to his childhood on Turkeyfoot Lake near Akron, Ohio, and remembered the many hours spent trying to hook five-pound largemouths. He grinned as he pictured using this technique in the highly populated resort area.

After several grenades the little men put on their uniforms and built a large fire. Jabbing green sticks in the mouths of the silver fish, they roasted them on the fire like marshmallows.

Bendell approached Nhual. "Ba Nua, I'm going over the hill for a few minutes and want to be alone."

"Trung-uy, your bodyguards have been ordered always to stay with you," Nhual said.

"I know, I know," Don replied. "But I need to be alone.

"I understand."

Don walked over the jungle-covered hill and went down into a small clearing. He walked through a primitive cemetery with wooden caskets in various stages of aging, some decomposed. Each was hand-carved from a tree and had a handle carved on each end. He walked to a smaller, brand-new one and knelt on one knee, eyes closed.

Opening misty eyes, he said, "Plar, I wanted to adopt and take you to America. I don't know which Vietnamese killed you, but I swear I'll make them pay."

He paused, choked up, then continued. "I love you, little Plar, and I'm glad at least that you're out of this godforsaken war. I swear to you I will help your people, and someday I'll make the world aware of what the Vietnamese have done to the Montagnards. I won't see you again in this world, so I won't come back here. 'Bye, Plar, I loved you.''

He turned and, clearing his throat, headed up the knoll. Before going over the top, he stopped, adjusted his green beret, pulled out a Swisher Sweet cigarillo, lit it, and replaced the invisible "macho mask." He disappeared over the top of the small ridge line.

The following morning found Bendell supervising the unloading of bags of rice off a C7A Caribou aircraft on the Dak Pek runway. His bodyguards were concerned, seeing a crowd of camp Vietnamese hanging around Bendell's jeep, but nobody saw the hands that had opened the gas tank and slipped something inside. They moved the milling Viets away from the jeep as Don signed the manifest and dropped a smoke grenade for the aircraft to lift-off.

Putting one of the striker cadres in charge of transporting the load of rice to the storage building, he hopped in the jeep and headed for the team house. Heading down the runway at forty-five miles per hour, he had to slow quickly for the dip at the blacktop's end.

Almost braking to a stop, Don downshifted the synchromesh four-speed into second gear and then dropped into first. Fortunately it was then that the explosion occurred. Subconsciously Bendell blessed whoever had cut the tops and windshields off Dak Pek's jeeps and removed the doors. He instantly dived to his left through a wall of flame. He hit the ground in a somersault and came up running, holding a minor bruise and scratch on his left forearm.

Legs shaking, but out of harm's way, the lanky officer sat down and watched his now blackened vehicle, totally engulfed in flame as it sent tongues of fire and black smoke shooting into the hot sky.

• • •

A few days later a FULRO cadre man at Dak Pek was poisoned by the Vietnamese. Hundreds of Dega attended his funeral, and the Americans on Bendell's team, as usual not knowing, thought it was just another dead Montagnard. The man, a friend of Bendell's, had not died alone; that night another friend, an important FULRO informant, one of several who listened to the LLDB through their team-house walls, had been beaten to death by a gang of Vietnamese wielding clubs.

The following night, Don was on radio watch in the U.S. team house. Everybody on the team took turns, half the nighttime hours per man, listening to the two AN-PRC-25 radios in the team house, one on air-to-ground frequency for aircraft, the other on ground-to-ground frequency to monitor company-size operations in the jungle.

He set his book down and petted the black-and-white mongrel puppy, Ambush, he had picked up in Nha Trang. His attention perked as the ground-to-ground crackled, but it was a far-off transmission from another unit.

Lighting a cigarette, he rose, stretched, and walked into the kitchen area, pouring another mug of coffee. Looking out the team-house door, he saw the sky lighten with false dawn. He stepped out into the morning chill and literally froze.

Something was wrong, and he sensed it. Slowly looking down, he saw his right green-and-black jungle boot resting atop a black trip wire. He didn't move. Buckets of sweat cascaded from his pores. His eyes followed the trip wire to a detonator attached to a cluster bomb unit, probably taken from the air strike on his first operation. Bendell figured that the trip wire either had not detonated, or there was a pressure-release device that would detonate when the tension was removed from the trip wire.

Carefully Don reached back inside the team-house door, grabbed his CAR-15, and slowly set it on top of the trip wire. He then worked up his courage, slowly lifted his foot, and dived behind the front wall of the team house.

Nothing happened. Breathing a sigh of relief, Bendell attached some commo wire from a roll in the team house to his weapon and yanked the wire. Still it did not explode.

Bendell alerted the team, and after daylight, everybody back at a safe distance, he shot the CBU with his CAR-15.

The resulting explosion sent clumps of dirt and gravel flying in the air and sent Don's imagination scurrying in all directions as he pondered the outcome had he not been protected once more.

With the adrenaline surge past and the subsequent letdown, he decided to retire to his bunker for at least part of the day. With his sensual and sexy lover, however, he couldn't consider rest. In fact, he was thinking of more explosions as he lay there, naked, running a fragrant, purple jungle flower all over Ning's well-muscled copper body. She sighed and whimpered as the soft blossom swirled erotically over her nipples, which grew taut and erect. Goose bumps rose on her skin as his lips replaced the purple flower.

They kissed long and deep, their tongues wrestling as if in hand-to-hand combat. Her pelvis rose as he continued running the flower down her body and between her legs, following it with gentle kisses.

He rolled on top of her and entered her, staring into her smiling eyes. His hips moved slowly up and down as they both stared deep into each other's soul and smiled warmly. His fingers ran through her raven hair and traced tiny circles on her cheeks and temples. Breathing heavier and biting their lips, they could not continue slowly as their pleasure mounted. Waves of ecstasy pounded in their loins as they lost themselves in their own passion.

"I love you one thou," Ning cried, panting heavily.

"I love you too," he gasped.

They came together simultaneously with orgasmic wave after wave like the pounding of the jungle from a massive

B-52 strike. Their bodies pushed together over and over until they both were drained.

They lay there quietly, still locked together, still staring into each other's eyes and planting light kisses on each other's faces and necks. He stuck the flower in her hair and, after fifteen minutes, rolled off her and lit a cigarette.

Scrunching her nose flirtingly, she grinned broadly and grabbed a half bottle of bourbon off his footlocker. Unscrewing the cap, she smelled it and held it up.

"How you drink?" Ning asked. "Is same-same as *hutt nhia*?"

Don laughed. "No, honey, it's not. Rice wine is smooth; this is napalm in your throat."

"So are you," she said seductively. "I try drink."

Taking a swig from the bottle, she started gasping, eyes bulging. She grabbed her throat and stomach, and he laughed at her but his eyes widened in horror as she continued thrashing, flopping onto the floor in pain and agony. Bendell grabbed her and held her, fighting panic, as he looked at the fallen woman.

"Oh, God! Oh, Ning!" he screamed helplessly. "Poison!"

He picked her up in his arms and she fainted.

Don and the new team medic stared skyward as the medevac helicopter took off with the moaning Montagnard beauty. Bendell clenched his teeth together in silent rage as he stepped into the jeep and drove toward the LLDB headquarters.

The camp commander, now Dai-uy Hoe, was eating rice and fish with his wife, young daughter, and four-year-old son. They all jumped as the door crashed open with a kick and Lieutenant Bendell stepped in, lighting a cigar with his best Eastwood imitation yet. Insecure and melodramatic he may have been, but there was no mistaking the hate and killing rage in the Green Beret's eyes.

Blowing a puff of smoke, Bendell said, "Your men have

been doing a lot of things lately to try to make my fellow team members lose face. It stops now.''

Then, as if it were an afterthought, he continued. ''Oh, yeah, thought you'd like to know, Dai-uy, that the medic thinks Ning didn't swallow enough poison to kill her.''

He rested his hand on his .357, then rubbed the little boy's head, an insult to the Vietnamese. He just glared at the dumbfounded commander.

''Pray to God she comes back alive.'' Don smiled and looked at Hoe's wife, then at his daughter and son, and added, ''Nice family you got here, Dai-uy.''

With that he backed out the door and walked off. The little boy swallowed a mouthful of rice and looked at the still open door.

''Cowboy,'' he said.

. . . 16 . . .

PRISONER AGAIN

Y Bham Enuol's eyes narrowed into slits and his face reddened with anger. "Ksor Kok, you are under arrest!"

"Under arrest?" Kok was flabbergasted. "What do you mean, under arrest, Mr. President? I have been totally loyal to you and the movement!"

"You young, foolish . . . How could you dare to accuse three of my most trusted advisers of being spies for the Yuan?" Y Bhan fumed. "You are confined to your quarters until I decide you have learned your lesson. If you were somebody else, you would be put to death for your treason!"

"Treason!" Kok raged. "Treason! Mr. President, those three are all from your tribe, the Rhade, and you won't listen to me because I am Jarai and young. They are spies for the Viets and are supposed to assassinate FULRO leaders. You have been blinded! You even encourage one of them to marry your daughter and they sold us out, but everybody's afraid to tell you!"

Jutting his jaw defiantly, Kok continued. "But I'm not! I am loyal to you! Now they tell you the CIA wants you to return to Vietnam, but that's not true. The Yuan want you there to kill you!"

"Get out of here!" Y Bham yelled. "Enough! You're under arrest!"

Kok walked to the door and said quietly, "It is sometimes easier, Mr. President, to see the jungle trail under somebody else's feet than to see it under our own. I have been done a great injustice, but my loyalty is still to you and our people—all tribes, not just the Rhade."

He turned and walked out the door, guards on each side. Y Bham stared at the door.

... 17 ...
TENACITY

The multitopped muddy-capped camp of Dak Pek towered in the background as Don, the assistant medic, and Suat tossed bars of Red Cross soap to dozens of villagers along the shore of the Dak Poko River. While the villagers laughed, the young officer grabbed a wrinkled, gray-haired village woman and led her out into the clear river. Bending the laughing grandmother over and splashing water on her, he took a bar of soap and scrubbed her back and then her breasts. The villagers howled with laughter, as did the old woman. The medic tossed a little Jeh boy in the river and started shampooing his hair with a bar of soap.

Bendell yelled, "Suat, tell them that this kills many of the evil things that make them get sick!"

Many Jeh started into the river, turning it into a giant communal bathtub.

Don climbed out of the water to get more soap and froze as he saw Ning walking toward him, a giant smile on her beautiful face. He smiled and walked toward her, marveling at the beauty of her face; the long, shiny black hair blowing in the wind; full, pert breasts bouncing. A pouring rainfall started as the two came together in a long, lingering kiss, trying to melt into each other's body. Finally they stepped back.

"How's your belly?" he asked.

Smiling, with tears welling, she replied. "Me better . . . but Vietnamese no stop try kill you. Kill friends you."

Don smiled and hugged her. "Don't worry, Ning. They won't kill any more of my friends, and they won't try to kill you again, I promise."

Just below the American hill and above the dispensary stood a long building. At the bottom end of the building was a storehouse for rice, indigenous rations, and uniforms. Before that was a large empty room that Don converted into a schoolhouse for the Dega children. At the end nearest the Americans was the barbershop.

The barber, a Vietnamese with five gold-capped teeth displayed in a continuous smile, was humming as he swept the floor, back to the door. There was a whoosh sound, followed by a twanging that was drowned out by his scream as he grabbed his now bleeding right ear. His scream was choked off as he stared at the bowie-size knife, still vibrating where it had stuck in the back wall. The big knife had two brass inlays in the back of the blade and numerous Jeh symbols engraved in the massive steel blade, forged from a piece of shrapnel from a five-hundred-pound bomb. The water-buffalo-horn handle was highly polished and made this particular knife unmistakable to everyone in the camp, including the barber.

He turned slowly, to stare into the taunting, menacing hazel eyes of Lieutenant Bendell, Eastwood glare and cigarillo firmly in place. Bendell grinned sadistically as the barber, bowing and smiling, literally wet himself.

Although everybody knew that Bendell spoke fluent Vietnamese, he now publicly refused to speak it, or to speak with any Vietnamese except through an interpreter.

Tieh, the camp's newest interpreter, recovered Bendell's knife and handed it to him. The bodyguards stood outside.

Bendell looked at the barber but spoke to Tieh. "Tieh, tell this greasy little bastard that I know he's not a real barber."

Tieh translated as the panic-stricken man just shook.

The lieutenant continued. "Tieh, ask him if he's a hit man from Kontum, hired by the Vietnamese to kill me."

Bendell quickly drew his .357 Magnum, cocking it, and pushed the barrel into the man's flaring nostril. By now the barber was near fainting, but he managed to shake his head yes. Don smiled and uncocked the gun, spinning it once backward into the holster.

"Tell him, 'Right answer. He lives for now.' Then tell him that I'll give him enough time to go to the LLVC and tell them what just happened." Don grinned and blew smoke into the man's face. "Then tell him that the next time I see him, I will shoot him on sight. In fact, I'll gut-shoot him just to hear him scream."

Tieh translated, and the man, drained with relief, moved quickly toward the door after Don shoved a cigarillo between the man's lips.

"Cam on, Trung-uy! Cam on, Trung-uy!" he said nervously, and then ran for the LLDB team house.

Throwing his arm around Tieh's shoulder, Don led him out the door and up the drive. "C'mon, Tieh, I'll buy ya a beer."

They walked into the new addition to the team house and saw Larry Crotsley, Commo Willy, and several other NCOs seated around the built-in, felt-topped poker table. Sergeant Crotsley was explaining to the others about the various layers of dirt, rocks, PSP, and so on, that extended down for twelve feet, covering the new TOC and commo bunker. He was excited as he explained how even deadly 220 rockets wouldn't be able to penetrate the TOC's depths.

Commo Willy, always cheerful, said teasingly, "Where you been, sir? Out drinking rice wine and eating rats and monkeys again?"

Bendell smiled as he opened a refrigerator with a sign on the door that read: REPENT, LEGS, GOD IS AIRBORNE. He got out two cans of beer, handing one to Tieh.

He then answered, "Commo Willy, there was a patrol walking through the jungle and they passed a beautiful jungle flower. The first guy was an American, and he thought, 'What a beautiful flower. I wish I could give it to my mother.'

"The second was a Vietnamese," Don continued, "and he thought, 'What a beautiful flower. I wonder what I could sell it to the American for?'

"The third guy was a Yard, and he thought to himself, 'I wonder what that tastes like?' "

... 18 ...

THE YUAN TRY AGAIN

Kok was seated behind the padded bar eating a slice of apple pie. A crumb dropped on his bartender's uniform as two U.S. Air Force sergeants walked in the door and sat at the bar. He set down the empty plate and smiled at them.

"That tastes good," he said enthusiastically. "What you sergeants want?"

One said, "How you doin'? How 'bout a beer and some blackjack?"

"Sure thing," Kok said, removing his apron. "I'm off now, but I'll tell the other bartender. Number-one?"

The other sergeant smiled. "Sure, number-one, Siu Ton. See ya tomorrow."

Smiling, Kok nodded and gave the order to the Vietnamese bartender, who had just walked behind the bar. He headed for the door, whistling.

Still using his phony name, he was working at the L19 Airport NCO Club in Ban Me Thuot. Y Bham had released him after three months of house arrest when he learned that Kok was correct about the three spies. Never again would Y Bham question the young, zealous Jarai. In fact, it wouldn't be long before Kok would become his chief of staff and the third in command of the secret Dega independence movement.

He thought of these recent events happily as he stepped out of the club and into the bright sunlight. Kok froze at the sound and sight of twenty guns being cocked and aimed at his head. He was completely surrounded by twenty armed Vietnamese military police, each ready to pull his trigger.

A second lieutenant brandishing a U.S. Army Colt .45 automatic stepped up to Kok. Kok stuck his hands in his pockets and gulped.

"What's wrong, Thieu-uy?" Kok asked in Vietnamese.

"Is your name Ksor Kok?" The lieutenant asked.

Making a face, Kok responded, "No, my name is Siu Ton."

"Let me see your identification," the officer demanded.

Using his left hand, Kok pulled out his wallet and handed it to him. The lieutenant examined the papers, then looked up. "We are taking you in for questioning."

Kok started to withdraw his right hand from his pocket, and said, "No . . . I"

He stopped as they all watched an Air Force jeep sliding to a halt near them. A U.S. Air Force sergeant was driving, but a Special Forces captain cheerfully stepped out of the passenger seat and walked up. The Vietnamese lieutenant saluted him, and he returned it.

"I noticed you questioning this Montagnard," the captain said, "and wondered what's going on, Lieutenant."

"Dai-uy, this man claims to be n-named Siu Ton," the Vietnamese officer said, stammering, "but we are sure he is a dangerous criminal named Ksor Kok."

"If he's a criminal," the Green Beret officer asked, "why is the military questioning him?"

"Well Dai-uy, uh . . . it is an internal matter."

"Well, Lieutenant," the captain replied, "I have just hired Siu Ton as an interpreter for my A-camp. Can he go with me and come to your office tomorrow?"

Flustered, the QC officer answered, "Well, uh . . . I . . . uh . . ."

Smiling, the captain grabbed his hand and motioned for Kok to get in the jeep. He shook the little man's hand vigorously.

"Thank you for your cooperation, Lieutenant," the captain said, hopping in the jeep. "I will tell your superiors."

The lieutenant started to speak, but the jeep sped away, the captain and sergeant laughing.

Sweating bullets, Kok pulled his right hand out of his pocket, breathed a sigh of relief, and carefully uncocked the .25 automatic he was holding.

"Thank you, Dai-uy," Kok said. "But you don't know me. Why did you help me?"

The American answered, "I saw that you were a Montagnard, and I know what the Vietnamese do to any Montagnard they take into custody. Soon as we're out of sight, I'll drop you off—and you better *di-di mau*. By the way, what is your name?"

"Does it really matter?" Kok said, grinning broadly. "You didn't know it when you helped me."

"Guess not," the captain replied. "Got anyplace to hide?"

"Yes, I have friends. I'll sneak out on a Beechcraft and won't be back," Kok said. "My wife waits for me. I want to thank you very much, Captain."

The jeep stopped. Kok jumped out, waved, and said, "God bless you."

"God bless you too," the captain replied, a strange look on his smiling face. "Good luck."

... 19 ...

DAK SEANG

Mortars again started raining on the nearby Special Forces A-camp at Dak Seang. Dak Pek was tucked away in the northwesternmost corner of II Corps along the Laotian border and the Ho Chi Minh Trail. The A-camp just north of it, Kam Duc, had been overrun earlier in the year when the NVA had attacked it with Soviet tanks. Prior to that, the camp due south of Dak Pek, Dak Sut, had been over-run, and to the southeast, Dak To was also overrun. In the fall of 1968, the 24th NVA Regiment hit Dak Seang, the next camp south of Dak Pek, with everything they had. The A-team and strikers miraculously repelled the attack. Afterward, numerous bodies of NVA "sappers," suicidal fanatics, were hung up in the barbed wire.

Afterward, the camp had been under siege for weeks. NVA mortar crews rained mortars on the camp whenever a helicopter arrived, so Dak Seang had to be resupplied by airdrop. C7A Caribous flew low over the camp, tail-gates open, dropping food and ammo by cargo parachutes. Chuck Challela had left Dak Pek earlier and was now a weapons man at Dak Seang.

Bendell and a new team member, a young E5 named Larry Vosen, had been on an operation northeast of Dak Seang for fifteen days. Bendell volunteered for them to go and help repel the NVA attacking Dak Pek's sister camp.

On the way to Dak Seang, they were socked in by monsoons. They couldn't get food resupply by chopper, so for several days they ate food from the jungle, supplied by their one hundred Jeh strikers.

A Vietnamese who was married to a Montagnard woman had been trying, through his wife, to get intelligence on FULRO activities around Dak Pek, so FULRO had marked him for assassination. Ironically he accidentally drowned when their operation attempted a dangerous river crossing through the swollen, whirling rapids of the Dak Poko River.

Three Dega crossed, and Larry Vosen volunteered to cross after the Yuan drowned. Bendell, knowing that a few more strikers would likely drown in the crossing, elected to wait until helicopters could get in for an airlift. They arrived and dropped off the Dak Pek strike force outside the besieged camp.

Mortars bursting outside, Bendell, followed by Vosen, burst in the door of Dak Seang's team house. A fifteen-day growth of beard and the same grungy tiger-suit uniform worn day and night for two weeks made the two soldiers look like rejects from the Bataan Death March.

Cigarillo between his lips, Bendell said, "Brought ya one hundred ass-kickin' Jeh warriors to help get the gooks off yer ass."

Smiling, Chuck Challela walked over and shook hands. "Hey, Lieutenant, how's it hangin'?"

"At half mast, Chuck." Bendell laughed. "How are you?"

"Great, sir," Chuck replied, and addressed the team members. "Guys, this is Lieutenant Bendell, my CA/PO XO up at Dak Pek. He's the one better known on the radio as Clint Eastwood. Heard you lost a guy trying to cross the river. Sorry."

Accepting a beer and a cigarette, Bendell shrugged it off. "Oh, it's okay. He was a Vietnamese from my camp.

Well, I gotta hand it to you guys—a few days ago I thought Dak Seang was history.''

"So did we," Chuck replied. "See all the bodies in our barbed wire?''

Laughing, Don said, "Yeah, nice decorations.''

Another sergeant pointed to a spot on the map and said, "We been gettin' all our supplies by airdrop. Every fuckin' time a chopper tries to land, the NVA has mortar crews all over this area that start pounding the shit out of us.''

"What about air strikes?" Don asked.

"We've tried, but the slimy motherfuckers hide, probably in reinforced bunkers on the reverse slope of this steep ridge line. On top of that, NVA antiaircraft shot down a medevac helicopter right here." He continued to point at the map. "They wounded and captured the pilot, but the rest of the crew got away and E and E'd back here through the jungle.''

"How 'bout it, Chuck," Don asked. "You've kicked a lot of ass. Wanna go kick some more?''

"Do Green Berets eat pussy?" Chuck grinned.

"That answers that," Bendell said as everyone laughed. "When do ya wanna leave?''

"How 'bout first light, Sir?''

"Sounds good to me," the officer answered, pointing to Larry across the room. "Got a young E5 with me that just came to Dak Pek.''

Chuck asked, "Been shot at yet?''

"Not yet.''

Getting serious, Chuck said, "Well, he's about to get his cherry popped, sir.''

Grinning, Don said, "Good. He'll handle it.''

"Okay, I'll bring sixty Yards and a virgin E5 from my camp," Chuck responded.

"Good," Bendell replied, "Gonna go set up a perimeter. See you in the morning.''

• • •

Like Dak Pek, the jungle surrounding Dak Seang had been cut away on all sides for a good distance. With only tanglefoot foliage and occasional trees for cover, the joint operation, heading north by northwest in the early-morning light, was easy prey to North Vietnamese mortar crews.

Not far outside of Dak Seang, Don and Chuck looked at each other as they heard two hollow *thunks* from the ridge line directly west of them. They sprang into action and started shouting orders to Montagnard strikers.

"Mortar! Mortar! Spread out!" Chuck yelled. "Lie down!"

Farther back, Don could hear Larry Vosen yelling similar orders.

Bendell yelled the same thing in Jeh, *"Mok che! Mok che! Brang! Oih! Oih!"*

Knowing that one round could wipe out several men grouped together at once, the Americans hurriedly tried to get the Jeh strikers to spread out. Then they lay down, waiting for the 82-mm mortars to hit.

Up to this point the twenty-two-year-old Bendell had been shot at on several occasions; survived a few assassination attempts by the Vietnamese; been wounded in the face by a bullet at Fort Dix, New Jersey, in a training accident; shot down in a helicopter; and cut on the thigh by a whiskey bottle in a fight. But he couldn't remember ever being as frightened as he was waiting for those two mortar rounds to hit. They exploded, spewing dirt on several strikers, but no one was hurt. The strikers got up and continued on. After five minutes two more rounds were fired. Five more minutes and two more were fired.

Don and Chuck called in 105 howitzer fire and 4.2-inch mortar fire on the enemy positions, but it seemed that there were several mortar crews moving around, so they couldn't be pinpointed.

For an hour the rounds came two at a time every five minutes. It seemed every man on the operation lost twenty pounds of sweat during that time. Finally, however, they reached the relative safety of the triple-canopy jungle.

Here was a world now familiar to Bendell. Jungle so thick that one saw only dark green in all directions. The steaming muddy earth covered with leaves, grass and vines pulled at one's legs and arms. Overhead, the leaves were so thick that daylight barely penetrated.

Taking a break, Bendell sent two Dak Pek volunteers out on a scout. Removing their boots, packs, hats, and tiger suits, the two FULRO warriors, already noted for their courage and stealth, headed west, clad only in loincloths.

Upon returning, they reported immediately to Bendell. Unseen, they had located some NVA in khakhi uniforms headed northwest on a trail and had followed them. While returning to the operation, spotting some more NVA who were covered with branches and leaves for camouflage, they dived into the undergrowth. Finishing their report to Nhual and Bendell, the two brave men put their uniforms back on. Bendell went over to Sergeant Challela.

"You were right. The gooks were hitting us from three different mortar positions," Bendell said, pointing to a map covered with combat acetate and grease pencil marks. "Here, here, and here—and even hiding in bunkers on this cliff. Those two Yards think we're gonna get hit moving along this saddle. Let's divide the Yards into three columns and sweep the saddle and then we'll move 'em on line if the point or main body gets hit."

"Sounds good, Trung-uy," Chuck said. "Don't forget, these little fuckers kicked a whole battalion from the Fourth Division off this ridge line in less than half an hour." He pointed at the map.

Sensing a chance for his macho Clint Eastwood facade, Bendell slowly lit a cigarillo and glared. "Yeah, and we're gonna run the little yellow bastards into Laos."

Sergeant Challela chuckled and slapped Bendell's shoulder. "Spoken like a true snake eater. Let's go kick some gook ass."

Still pointing at the map, Don said, "We're gonna get hit somewhere along here, I'll bet."

"I'll be ready," the olive-skinned sergeant said.

Half an hour later, the silence of the jungle roaring in the lieutenant's ears, the world exploded into a symphony of hate. Hiding in camouflaged foxholes and spider holes, a platoon of NVA ambushed the Americans' point team. The NVA detonated captured American claymore mines, and the lead strikers were raked with a hail of withering automatic weapons fire from AK-47 rifles and an RPG machine gun. Everybody flattened.

Leaves and twigs dropping off surrounding trees and bushes and scattering on the ground around him, Bendell crawled over to Chuck Challela. The noise was deafening as automatic weapons fired, along with hand grenades and claymore mines. The NVA screamed taunts while firing.

Chuck and Bendell jumped up, and Don yelled over the gunfire, "Get your E5 and take the left! Larry and I will take the right! Let's assault on-line and sweep the whole ridge line!"

Giving Bendell the thumbs-up sign, Chuck yelled, "Fuckin' A!" and ran off.

Nhual ran to Don, who yelled, "Nhual, let's get 'em up and assault on-line and get our men yelling too! Let's outshout 'em!"

"All right, Trung-uy!" Nhual yelled back, crawling off with bullets cracking overhead.

Seeing enemy muzzle flashes and NVA wearing branches and leaves, moving around a lot, Bendell moved back and forth, getting strikers up and moving forward. Crouching and running to the right, he ran into Larry Vosen.

He yelled above the overwhelming noise, "Larry, our point got hit! Get 'em up and assault on-line! You take the right flank of the line!"

"Willco!" Larry yelled.

Larry immediately started moving strikers back and

forth on-line. Within seconds a cry of *Allez!''* rose up in unison among the strike force. Moving forward and gaining confidence, they fired at the enemy and outshouted them with a continuing cry of *''Allez!''* The NVA, spirits breaking, began a retreat.

Sweeping along the ridge line, the strikers near Bendell passed through a stand of hardwoods, where the thick undergrowth thinned out dramatically. One of Bendell's bodyguards—a small, wiry, old Jeh with five grown sons—moved over to his left, passing in front of the American. Simultaneously he was hit with a burst of AK-47 fire, and an NVA in a camouflaged foxhole detonated a claymore mine, knocking down Bendell and the Montagnard. The bodyguard was riddled with bullets and pellets. The canteen was even blown off Bendell's hip, but miraculously he hadn't been hit by a single pellet. He ran to the bleeding Jeh and, pulling a green metal can from his rucksack, summoned help.

Bendell yelled, "Medic, Bac Si! Bac Si!"

While a couple of American-trained Jeh medics ran over, Bendell opened the green can and pulled out a glass bottle, a tube, and an IV needle. He tied off a long vein in the man's forearm and inserted the large needle, starting the blood expander, serum albumin, going. In the meantime, the medics attended his wounds.

Bendell looked at the severely wounded man. He smiled weakly up at the tall American. Don patted his shoulder and rose. Looking around, he saw several more dead. Walking along and firing, he started calling in and adjusting 105 howitzer and 4.2-inch mortar fire to the west, the direction in which the NVA were retreating. He also requested a tactical air strike.

Firing again, Bendell saw the little old Jeh's nephew, another of his bodyguards, go down. Still fighting, he reappeared a few minutes later, claymore pellets in both legs and one eye shot out. Incredibly, he was carrying another wounded Jeh striker. He smiled at Bendell, who pulled out a little cigar and stuck it between the warrior's lips and lit it.

Chuck Challela ran up through the smoke and earsplitting din, dragging the young E5 from Dak Seang by the arm.

Trying to yell above the shooting, Chuck, red-faced, screamed, "Sir, I told this yellow fucker to take a platoon and secure that LZ I cut last week for dust-offs to come in, and he refuses to do it!"

Without hesitating, Bendell ejected his empty magazine from his CAR-15, inserted another magazine into the weapon, and jacked a round into the chamber. He thumbed the safety to full automatic and jammed the barrel under the E5's chin.

"I don't argue in combat, you fuckin' pussy!" Bendell yelled. "Move out and do your job before I count five or I'll kill you! Right now!"

Scared to death, the E5 pleaded, "I don't wanna get killed, sir! I—"

Bendell interrupted him. "One! Two!"

Eyes bulging, the E5 ran toward the LZ, grabbing a few Montagnards on the way. Chuck grinned at the lieutenant.

"Thanks, sir!" Chuck yelled.

Serious, Bendell shouted back, "If he balks any more, shoot him! We can't afford for others to be killed because of him!"

"Be glad to!" Challela replied, and ran off.

Finally the firing petered out and the drone of a plane could be heard overhead. The jungle canopy was so thick, the aircraft couldn't be seen.

Don grabbed the radio. Pointing and yelling at Nhual, he said, "The LZ's that way. Let's get the wounded over there!" Then, speaking into the radio, he said, "Bird Dog, this is Kansas Oxfly Alpha, over."

The voice Don identified as that of a bald-headed, smiling Air Force lieutenant colonel with a handlebar mustache crackled through the radio: "Kansas Oxfly Alpha, this is Bird Dog two-three, over."

"Two-three, Alpha," Don continued. "I'm gonna shoot a pyrotechnic through the canopy and mark our position, over!"

"Roger, Alpha, I'm watchin'. Got two jets on-station, ready to drop some ordnance, over."

Don prepared a hand-held parachute flare and tried to aim it through a hole in the jungle canopy. Striking the bottom of the olive-drab tube with his right hand, he fell and screamed in pain as the device exploded. Reaching into a pouch on his belt, he pulled out an Army bandage and tightly wound it around his right wrist and hand. Nhual handed him another parachute flare, which he fired left-handed, banging the triggering device bottom down on his left knee. The flare exploded up through the canopy, then fired open, a big nylon parachute opening up above it.

Using his left hand, Bendell fired the last round in his magazine, ejected, tossed the magazine down the front of his shirt, and loaded another. His shirt now clanged as he moved with ten empty magazines inside it.

"Alpha, two-three," the forward air controller said over the radio, "I see a green flare, over."

Into the radio Bendell said, "Two-three, Alpha, that's me. Kick their ass, man, over."

"Gladly. Don't move any farther west of your current position, over," the FAC said.

"Wilco," Bendell said. "We're headed to the LZ to get our wounded out of here, out."

The small, old bodyguard was still alive. Two medics worked on his wounds as Don gave him mouth-to-mouth resuscitation. Nhual ran up.

"Trung-uy," Nhual said angrily, "see the Vietnamese medic over there?"

Between breaths, Bendell gasped "Yeah" as he raised his eyes.

Nhual pointed at the dying bodyguard. "The son of a

bitch refused to give him mouth-to-mouth because he is Montagnard.''

"He's breathing," Bendell said, rising up. "Okay, Nhual, I'll take care of it later."

Chuck, in the middle of the chopped-down jungle clearing, was talking on the radio and looking out to the east at a circling Huey helicopter with a red cross in a white circle on its side. The sergeant, fuming, slammed the mike down and looked over at the lieutenant.

"Hey, Lieutenant," Chuck yelled as Don started toward him, "the fucking dust-off won't land cause he said that we haven't been out of contact long enough!"

Bendell stormed over to the radio and picked up the mike.

"The fucks!" he said to Chuck. "We're trying to rescue their buddy and they won't land to pick up our wounded. I always thought dust-offs had balls!"

He said into the radio, "Dust-off, this is Kansas Oxfly Alpha, over."

The radio voice said, "Go, Alpha, over."

Tight-lipped, Don said, "You know the size of my unit, over?"

"Negative," the pilot replied. "Over."

"Well, it's a large one, and all of my men are aiming at you right now," Bendell replied, "and I'm gonna shoot you out of the sky if you don't pick up my wounded right now, you cowardly fuck, out!"

Chuck started laughing as the dust-off banked sharply toward the landing zone. Bendell stomped away.

"You're definitely SF, sir," Chuck said with a laugh.

Don looked back, a scowl on his face, and broke into a laugh. Then he returned to the bodyguard. The man grabbed Bendell's hand and grinned.

"Trung-uy, me die," the tightly muscled old man said. "Go see Jesus now."

Misty-eyed, Don smiled. "Tell Jesus that Trung-uy say he's number-one."

The bodyguard said weakly, "Family me?"

Bendell smiled. "No sweat."

Still smiling, the bodyguard's head fell to the side, eyes staring blankly. Bendell watched, dumbfounded, as two strikers grabbed him and tossed his body on the medevac helicopter that had just landed. He stared as the wounded's packs and rifles were dropped on the bodyguard's face and body. Several of the wounded also were placed on top of the still form, and the dust-off quickly lifted off.

Snapping out of it, the hazel-eyed young officer put a cigar in his mouth and lit it. He walked over to Nhual.

"Ba Nua, where's that Yuan medic?" Don asked.

"In the trees with the LLDB team sergeant," Nhual answered, pointing.

Bendell, followed by Nhual, walked over to a group of four Vietnamese, squatting and laughing at the jungle's edge. He grabbed the medic, pulled him up by his hair, and spun him around. The angry commando kicked him in the groin and then flattened him with an uppercut. He turned and walked away as the other three stared at him in shocked silence.

"Saddle up and move out!" Don ordered. He stalked forward, jaw set, as Chuck walked up beside him.

"You know what, Sergeant Challela?" Don said.

"What, Lieutenant?"

"War sucks!"

Chuck Challela, Larry Vosen, and eight Montagnards walked up out of the jungle and entered the company perimeter. Larry stopped at a fire with Nhual and poured a cup of coffee. Chuck walked over to Bendell and dropped his heavy harness at the edge of an NVA circular antiaircraft position dug into the ground. From their vantage point high atop a mountain, Dak Seang could easily be seen five miles to the east and three thousand feet down. It had been two days since the big firefight.

Bendell disgustedly threw the radio's microphone on the ground.

"Patrol didn't find much, Trung-uy," Chuck said, and took an offered cup of hot coffee from Don.

Ignoring the comment, Bendell said, "Were you monitoring your radio?"

"No, sir."

"That slimy little son of a bitch from higher headquarters just took credit for everything we did," Bendell said, fuming. "And the CO from the First Brigade, Fourth Division, at Dak To just told him he's getting a Silver Star." Don was pacing now. "He's on his way out here on a chopper so he can greet their dust-off when it picks up the pilot's body we recovered."

Chuck sipped his coffee as he stared at the pilot's body on the stretcher. Next to him lay the twisted wreckage of a medevac helicopter, radios, and stripped-away valuables. The man's arms were outstretched and the back of his skull was missing. An AK-47 round was right between his eyes, and another bullet had gone through both thighs, which had been bandaged.

"You see what they did to this poor fucker?" Chuck asked.

"Broke every joint in his body," Don answered.

"Then shot him between the eyes," Chuck added.

"Should've been the asshole from high headquarters," Bendell said, then paused, rubbing his month-old beard. "Maybe it will be."

He poured a cup of coffee and continued. "Fuck, I'm ready to go home, man."

... 20 ...

THE PLEI TRAP VALLEY

Ksor Kok stood on the runway at Dak Pek with Bayh, Suat, Tieh, and several other Montagnard leaders. He carried an M16 and a small bag. Larry Crotsley and a strongly built captain with glasses also stood by the runway. The sound of ten approaching Huey helicopters reverberated through the valley as all eyes looked southward. The captain tossed out two green smoke grenades, one near and one far, as the lead chopper came into view.

The helicopters, flying in perfect formation, dropped and touched down on the blacktop runway, spewing their contents—a company of grungy, dirty, bandaged strikers—in all directions. Bendell and Larry Vosen hopped out and ran over to Larry Crotsley and the crew-cut captain, and all four shook hands. Bendell, his right wrist bandaged, shook with his left hand. He ran over to Kok and the Dega leaders. He and Kok shook hands, and Don walked him to one of the choppers. Bendell spoke briefly to the pilot as Kok showed the man his travel papers. The pilot nodded, and Kok again shook with Bendell and jumped·on the chopper. He waved as the rotary-wing aircraft lifted off and, turning, roared out of sight. Bendell returned to the Americans. All four jumped in the jeep with the captain, Joe Dietrich, the new team commander, driving.

"Welcome back, you two," Joe said. "How'd you like Dak Seang?"

"No thanks, sir," Bendell replied. "I'd rather forget it."

Joe laughed. "You know we were listening on the radio when that chair-borne ranger sitting on his ass took credit for what you did."

"What is it you say, Captain?" Bendell said. "Medals are for Boy Scouts. We're warriors. Fuck 'em!"

"How you like it here at Dak Pek, Captain?" Larry Vosen asked. "Better than Plei Me?"

Joe replied, "A lot easier to defend. You guys starved? Chow's ready. Sergeant Vosen, I heard you handled yourself very well under fire."

"He sure did, sir," Don responded. "I gotta go take care of something over at Bravo Company with Nhual."

Joe stopped, and Bendell hopped out and started toward his bunker. "See you guys in a while," he said.

A short time later, showered, shaved, and in clean jungle fatigues, numerous bracelets jangling on his wrists and his right wrist wrapped in a clean Ace bandage, Bendell stood before a small, wrinkled Jeh woman. Her five grown sons stood behind her, and Nhual stood at Don's side.

Nhual spoke as the woman listened, tears glistening in her eyes. "She says you bring her much honor by coming to her."

Smiling warmly, Don said, "Tell her, Ba Nua, that I am honored to speak with her."

Bendell took her hands as Nhual translated and then said, "Tell her that when her husband died, he grabbed my hand and said he would see Jesus."

"I already told her, first thing," Nhual said.

"Tell her that her husband got shot and hit by a claymore because he was saving me," Don said, "and I will never forget him."

Nhual translated quickly, and Don tried to understand her response.

"She says that was his job," Nhual said. "and that he loved you."

"Tell her he did his job great and was my best body-guard. Tell her also that her nephew is a great bodyguard too," Bendell continued. "Tell her he had his eye shot out and claymore pellets in his legs and still helped carry the wounded to the medevac."

Nhual, again speaking too quickly for Don to under-stand, translated and spoke for a long time with the woman. Eyeing Bendell, she chuckled along with her sons.

"Ba Nua, what in the hell did you say?"

Grinning, Nhual said, "What you said."

"What else?"

"I told her that a Vietnamese medic refused to give mouth-to-mouth to her husband and you kicked and punched him and knocked him out. I also tell . . . I mean, I told her you gave him mouth-to-mouth and put IVs in both arms but could not save him."

Don bent over and pulled bolts of colored cloth, beads, and thread from a bag, handing them and a large wad of dong, the Vietnamese currency, to her. The woman's black eyes welled up with tears, and she addressed Nhual. In the background, her five sons stood a little straighter and puffed their chests out a little farther.

"She says before enemy ever kills Trung-uy," Nhual translated, "first she and her five sons will die."

"I . . . I . . . ah," Bendell said, stammering, "let's go, Ba Nua."

He bowed and hugged her and left the bunker.

Barefoot, Ning was wearing Levi's jeans and a T-shirt as she and Don sat side by side in the sun atop a sand-bagged bunker. He wore cutoff fatigue pants, sandals, his .357, and his Yard knife.

Several Montagnard children played around them, run-ning up to tickle Don. He reached out and grabbed a screaming, giggling four-year-old; turned him upside down; and tickled his ribs as they all laughed.

Don spoke to the children. "Okay, *mi chiu . . . mi chiu*!"

They ran off. He turned his head and stared into Ning's smiling eyes. She stared back lovingly.

"How long you stay?" she asked. "Go home America?"

"With the Dega," he said, looking out at the broad green valley, "I don't know, Ning. Maybe forever."

"How can you?" she said. "America is number-one thou!"

"That's why," he replied quickly, "your people deserve America, not being slaughtered into extinction by the Vietnamese."

"Me don't know words but understand you speak," Ning responded. "Don, I love you too many."

"I love you too many too," Don said.

Joe Dietrich pulled up in the jeep, smiling. "Hop in, Bendell. Got a Caribou coming in."

Don jumped in the jeep and Joe turned and drove toward the runway. "You ever going to get your paperwork caught up?" he asked.

"I'd like to, sir," Don answered, "but I've been going out on back-to-back operations ever since I've been here."

Joe grinned. "You'd make a lousy secretary."

"Yes, sir."

"What are you going to do about Ning?" Joe asked.

"What about her?"

"I mean," Joe said, "didn't you get married right before 'Nam?"

"Yes, sir," Don said angrily. "After all those back-to-back operations I got called in to Kontum and got my ass chewed by Colonel Marquis for not writing enough letters to my wife. She had contacted the Red Cross."

Joe grinned. "Isn't your anger a little misdirected? Shouldn't you hate the enemy and not your wife?"

"Fuck, I don't hate her," Don said resignedly. "I hate what's happening to the Yards. You don't understand, sir. Nobody does. All the Americans love the Yards. Some want to pity them, some want to baby-sit them 'cause they think they're ignorant and backward, but nobody really tries to understand them."

Don lit a cigarette and continued. "Nobody knows what's really happening here, besides the war."

Joe laughed. "We talking about FULRO?"

Don grinned. "Now, sir, you know we aren't to mention that word."

"Yeah, I know," Joe said. "What are your plans?"

"Well, I'm staying."

"Here? How long?" Joe asked.

"Until the war's over and maybe then some," Don replied. "These people need help. My extension's been approved. When I leave here, I requested going to the Mike Force or CCN."

"What the hell you want to go to SOG for?" Joe asked.

"A lot of my buddies are there," Don said.

"Dead or captured?" Joe asked. "Don't volunteer for CCN. They'll probably send you, anyway. Maybe when you go on your thirty-day extension leave, you'll calm down a little, if you get a chance to get back to the world for a few weeks."

"What do you mean, 'calm down'?" Don asked.

"You have a lot of rage in you. You might be too close to the Yards," Joe said seriously. "Some of the guys on the team are afraid of you—especially in the morning, before you've had a drink."

Inside, Don wanted to scream, and he felt his ears burning.

Changing the subject and lightening the mood, Joe said, "I'm taking a hundred strikers to Polei Klang for a joint operation. We're going to invade the Plei Trap Valley."

"Shit," Don said eagerly, "that's an NVA stronghold."

"Not only that," Joe said. "NVA's infiltrating through

there with Soviet tanks and trucks. They've got a road built—with underwater bridges even—and maybe a POW camp with American prisoners in it. I need a good number-two man.''

Excited and enthused, the lieutenant asked, "When do we leave?"

With his .357 Magnum Don, in his tiger suit, was shooting cans being tossed up in the air. In the background was the A-camp of Polei Klang. In the direction across the broad valley were some jungle-covered mountains, and right next to the operation's base camp was a mechanized infantry unit from the Fourth Infantry Division. Nhual and several other Montagnards were also taking turns shooting at the cans.

Seeing an opportunity to make the hated lieutenant lose face, a young LLDB sergeant from Dak Pek walked up, several Vietnamese backing him up. It was rumored that this brat's crooked, wealthy father had bought him his stripes and that he had been the biggest troublemaker on the LLDB team since arriving at Dak Pek. He was also wearing an Army Colt .45 automatic on his right hip.

Sensing something was in the wind, Bendell reloaded his revolver and spun it backward into his quick-draw holster. Trying to appear relaxed, he had every sense tensed and ready for trouble. This was all completely sparked by the cocky grin on the face of the young Vietnamese.

The American cowboy was the biggest hero of the Vietnamese soldiers. Vietnamese punks tried to imitate cowboys and practiced quick-draw for hours. The brat NCO was one of those.

Obviously showing off for his grinning Vietnamese friends and trying to make Bendell lose face, the sergeant stopped in a gunfighter's crouch twenty feet in front of Bendell.

He said, "Trung-uy, you—me have showdown same-same cowboy."

There it was. In a split second Don realized several things: One, the sergeant was positive the American wouldn't take him seriously and would back down, losing face; two, the sergeant had a heavy, bulky .45 auto to draw, while he had a .357 Magnum revolver in a quick-draw holster; three, Don had grown up with heroes like the Range Rider, Roy Rogers, and the Lone Ranger and had practiced quick-draw, like many American boys since kindergarten.

Without hesitation Bendell stood facing the Vietnamese, pulled out a cigarillo, and played his best Eastwood role.

Grinning, he said, "Okay, Trung-si. Nhual will count to five in Vietnamese. When he says *nam*"—the word for *five*—"we draw and fire . . . and you die. Count, Nhual."

Nhual said, *"Mot . . . hai . . ."*

In a panic, the Vietnamese put his hands up, pleading, "No, wait! Stop! I joke you!"

"Keep counting, Nhual," Bendell said, squinting over the Swisher Sweet.

"Ba . . . bon . . ." Nhual went on.

In a panic, the LLDB NCO clawed for his gun before Nhual got to five, and the tall American dived straight forward, drawing at the same time. His revolver came out smoothly, thumb cocking the hammer. At the same time his left hand came out and grabbed his right hand, the gun's grip providing extra support. He looked along the sights and instinctively thought, Fire at center mass, as he had been trained. He tightened his stomach and diaphragm as his body and elbows struck the ground. Looking atop the sights, Don could see the center of the man's chest as he was still pulling the .45 automatic out of his holster.

The realization suddenly hit the profusely sweating NCO as he let go of the gun and stared wide-eyed at Bendell's gun barrel. Grinning and enjoying the sound of several Dega chuckling, Don kept aiming at the sergeant's chest. The NCO turned as white as a Persian cat eating cotton candy in a blizzard. As Bendell got up, still aiming at the

NCO's midsection, he walked slowly forward until the barrel was six inches from the man's navel.

"Trung-si," Bendell said, cigar between his lips, "you ever try to make me lose face again, I'll kill you."

The .357 Magnum came up and smashed the LLDB sergeant across the bridge of his nose, cartilage giving way with a crunch. The man fell back against his buddies and four Vietnamese lay on the ground as the Jeh warriors roared with laughter. Don turned, noticed his six silent shadows lowering their rifles, and grinned when he realized the rich brat would have lost no matter what.

Don walked to his canteen and took a very long drink of water and two salt pills, while the laughing Jeh warriors started throwing cans up and shooting at them once more. He knew that he had gone up another notch in their eyes. He also knew that the diarrhea cramps and nausea would pass in a few minutes if he ignored them. His legs were still shaking, but he knew no one could tell.

Hearing a jeep roar up, he turned and saw a Fourth Division second lieutenant driving from the mechanized infantry unit that was bivouacked next to his. Don dropped his canteen on his jungle hammock and walked over. The red-faced second lieutenant jumped out of the jeep in a rage. His Spec Four (Specialist Fourth Class) driver sat behind the wheel, suppressing a grin.

The "leg" officer screamed, "Cease fire! Cease fire!"

Nhual translated, and the Dega stopped shooting. Bendell—in a tiger suit with no insignia, a black scarf, and a camo cowboy hat—walked up.

"Can I help you, Lieutenant?" Don asked innocently. "You from that mech infantry unit?"

"Yes, I am!" he screamed. "Who's in charge here?"

"I am," Don said calmly.

"Soldier, you and your men are shooting up my LRRP patrol on that mountain!" he yelled, pointing. "What the hell do you think you're doing!"

"We're killing time, and there's no fucking way we're

shooting your LRRPs," Don said laughing. "That mountain's two miles away and covered with triple-canopy jungle."

"Who authorized you to fire a weapon, soldier?" the young officer screamed.

Laughing still, Bendell said dryly, "Congress, dickhead; we're at war, in case you hadn't noticed."

Still yelling, the lieutenant raged on. "I had to call in and get a grid clearance yesterday to shoot a rabid dog!" Even more red-faced, the veins in his neck and forehead almost bursting, he continued. "You can't just shoot when you want!"

Really laughing now, Don replied, "No wonder we're losing this cluster-fuck war!"

"Who are you, smart aleck?" the irate young officer fumed. "Who's your commanding officer?"

"I am, Lieutenant," Joe Dietrich said with authority.

The lieutenant snapped his head around to spot Joe walking up.

"Captain Joseph K. Dietrich, Operational Detachment A-242, Company B, Fifth Special Forces Group."

Don started grinning as the now embarrassed second lieutenant snapped to attention and saluted. Joe also wore a tiger suit and a Colt .41 revolver in a quick-draw holster, which he had taken from a dead Vietcong commander.

"Don't salute me in a combat zone, you asshole!" Joe snapped. "You might just as well put a bull's-eye on me!"

"Yes, sir," the lieutenant replied. "This soldier was very—"

Joe interrupted, "Lieutenant, this soldier is a first lieutenant who is due for promotion to captain shortly and who could also eat you for breakfast."

The lieutenant started to speak, couldn't, then mumbled, jumped in the jeep, and drove off, leaving Don and Joe laughing heartily.

They walked to the fire and sat down, both accepting canteen cups of hot chocolate from Nhual.

"What's the word, sir?" Bendell asked.

"Another delay," Joe replied disgustedly. "No air support. The Twelfth Tactical Fighter Wing in Cam Ranh Bay and the Thirty-first Tactical Fighter Wing from Tuy Hoa are both nailed down by typhoons."

"And the Viet commanders need time to warn the NVA before we go into Plei Trap Valley," Don replied angrily. "I can't believe I put in for an extension."

"Oh, come on, Don, admit it," Joe said teasing, "you're having a lot of fun, aren't you?"

Chuckling, Don said, "With all due respect, sir, I would just like to say . . ." Don stood up and lifted his leg and flatulated.

Joe laughed and said, "Here, here. You know officers never have gas."

Don fought back the old panicky feelings as the gas burned his eyes, throat, and lungs. Panic was already registering on the faces of his ten-man patrol of Montagnards. He heard the distinctive hiss and pop of a second NVA throwing a second gas grenade on the hillside to his left. The Yards started running down the enemy-constructed road in total fear and panic. Knowing that they could well be running straight into an NVA ambush, Don had flipped his CAR-15 to automatic and fired bullets, kicking up dirt at the feet of the lead Jeh.

"*Dei chiu!*" Don yelled. "Nhual, tell them not to panic! Don't run! We'll get ambushed!"

"*Mi dei chiu!*" Nhual screamed. "*Yuan cong-san chop bal hay!*"

Don continued, his eyes burning. "It's CS gas, Nhual! It won't kill us!"

"*Hang ku wia!*" Nhual yelled. "*Dei chiu*, you fucking cowboys!"

Proudly, eyes burning and watering, and fighting panic, the little patrol moved forward down the road, rifles at the ready. Don called in an artillery concentration on the hillside.

Joe Dietrich had become the first American who was not a prisoner of war to set foot in the Plei Trap Valley in years. Five companies of CIDG and Fourth Division units had air-assaulted into the longtime NVA stronghold, with Dak Pek assigned the westernmost sector. Joe had been in the lead helicopter and was the first man out and onto the landing zone.

They had been in the valley several days and had discovered many "treasures." With tac air, 175- and 155-mm howitzers, and Cobra and HUEY gunships in support, it was a tactician's wet dream.

Like numerous SF before them, Don and Joe had both dreamed of an opportunity not only to serve with distinction but maybe win a Medal of Honor, DSC (Distinguished Service Cross), or whatever. More importantly they dreamed of locating and freeing American POWs reportedly being held in the Plei Trap Valley.

Unfortunately numerous delays gave the NVA the opportunity to move the prisoners a few miles west into Cambodia.

When Don and the patrol got gassed, they were returning from Cambodia. They had wandered there, discovering a regimental headquarters, complete with woven bamboo barracks, latrines, and concrete-reinforced bunkers. Two armed Cobra helicopters flew overhead, complaining to Bendell that he had illegally crossed the dotted line and should return. He had been too busy taking photographs with his Minolta spy camera and was later told by S2 that his pictures had been sent to Paris.

An hour after the gas incident he was talking to Joe on the PRICK 25 (AN-PRC-25 radio) and checking out a two-thousand-kilo Soviet truck that he and his patrol had captured.

Joe's voice crackled over the radio. "Lackey Bravo, did you get the manufacturer's plate off it yet, over?"

"Lackey Alpha, this is Bravo, that's a big Rodge," Bendell replied, looking at a four-inch by four-inch stamped metal plate, "All the writing is in French, but it says that it was manufactured in Moscow in 1962. It's a two-thousand-kilo truck it says, over."

"Good job, Bravo," Joe replied. "The boss in P City wants you to stay there and secure the truck. He's sending a Chinook in to hook it out, over."

This operation was being run by the Fourth Infantry Division, and Dak Pek was working Opcon, or under Operational Control, of that unit. Don knew that Joe was letting him know that the commanding general of the Fourth Infantry Division in Pleiku wanted this captured NVA truck. He also knew that he and ten men were out in the open in a large, defoliated area and were supposed to guard a war trophy. He was very angry.

"Alpha, Bravo, we're in a hornet's nest and will damn sure get stung if we sit around smoking," Don said angrily. "What the hell's he want it for, over?"

"Bravo, Alpha," Joe answered. "Probably put in front of his Hotel Quebec. You don't argue with stars. Set up a perimeter and be careful, over."

In Bendell's frame of mind he probably would gladly have argued with a general; however, Joe had just given him a direct order. Joe was his CO and he was SF, and arguing further was out of the question, so he did what he had always done when frustrated. He grinned.

"Peewee Lackey Alpha, this is Bravo, Willco," Don said. "Alpha, if you hear some explosions, I have an under-stream bridge to blow up and a couple of bunkers, too, over."

Laughing, Joe knew what Bendell had in mind and replied, "Roger, Bravo, understand. Hey, we're getting worldly. I just captured some ammunition from Czechoslovakia, out."

The young commando removed his rucksack and pulled out several blocks of what looked like modeling clay and a container of blasting caps. He signaled two Yards, who carried disposable bazookas, M-72 LAWs, which were light antitank weapons.

He released the pin and pulled open the first LAW, plastic sight popping up, and placed it over his right shoulder. Making sure nobody was in the back-blast area, he aimed and grinned.

"Ba Nua," he said, "the CG of the Fourth Division wants us to stand around risking our lives protecting this communist piece of shit, so he can put it on the front lawn of his headquarters." He lit a cigarette. "Do you suppose there could be some NVA still hiding in it?"

Grinning, Nhual replied, "Could be, Trung-uy."

"Better not take any chances," Don replied, squeezing the trigger.

The deadly little rocket exploded through the door of the cab. Don, laughing, took the second LAW and repeated the procedure. He next took two HE grenades and pulled the pins.

"Get back!" Don laughed and told Nhual, "There may be a gook hiding in the cab."

He trotted up to the truck, tossed the grenades in the window, and sprinted away, diving on the ground, arms over his head. The doors and windows blew out with the explosion. Don and the patrol sat up, laughing.

"Nhual, there might be a VC hiding under the truck," Don said, still grinning. "Will you bring me that C-4 on my ruck, please?"

Nhual took the C-4, blasting caps, and a couple of pieces of time fuse to Bendell, who had walked over to the mangled vehicle. Within a minute Don had rigged both blocks of explosive under the truck on the frame.

Joe's company perimeter girded a lightly wooded hilltop. He had just boiled a canteen cup full of water and was pouring it into a thick, clear plastic bag of dehydrated chili con carne from a LRRP ration when he heard Bendell's voice come over the radio.

"Peewee Lackey Alpha, this is Lackey Bravo, on our way back. The big bird hooked the star-toter's trophy and oughta be flying over you shortly, out."

Joe reached over and keyed his mike twice to let him know he'd heard but was busy. Seconds later he heard the far-off *pop-pop* of an approaching Chinook helicopter. He started watching skyward and soon fell over laughing, spilling his chili. Above him, the Chinook passed, carrying the green, mangled piece of twisted steel, canvas, and rubber that used to be a two-thousand-kilo truck.

That night Don, Nhual, and Joe sat around a small fire drinking coffee and talking.

"Yes, sir, Commo Willy was on the radio when Lieutenant Leopold got captured at Ben Het," Don said. "The radio operator had his lower jaw shot off and was still transmitting."

"He was SF," Joe mused.

"Fuckin' A," Bendell replied. "Six Yards escaped a few days later and made it back to Ben Het. They said that Leopold had been shot through the thighs and that the gooks carried him into Laos in a barbed-wire cage. They were kept at an old French fort, and they said Soviet tanks kept driving in all day and all night."

"Son of a bitch," Joe said.

"Hey, Nhual, don't stare into the flames," Don said.

"How come, Trung-uy?" Nhual asked.

"Makes you night-blind," he replied. "Screws you up if you have to get into action quickly."

"You learn that at Bragg?" Joe asked, sipping his coffee.

"No, sir, American Indian trick. Never look directly at the flames. I'm goin' home. 'Night, captain . . . Ba Nua."

" 'Night, Bendell," Joe said.

"Good night, Trung-uy," said Nhual.

Bendell dumped out the rest of his coffee and cautiously made his way along the inside of the company perimeter. Almost out of sight in the darkness, six shadows glided along, paralleling him. Passing by a campfire, he was waved over by a Vietnamese civilian, Mr. Ho, who sat on a log by the smart-ass LLDB sergeant.

"Ciao Trung-uy, manh jioi?" Ho said.

"You know English, Ho," Bendell said, exasperated. "What do you want?"

Ho motioned for Bendell to sit down, so he squatted down Vietnamese style.

"Just want talk few minutes Trung-uy" came the toothy reply.

"So talk."

"Why are you here?" Ho asked seriously.

"Where?" Bendell queried. "Plei Trap?"

"No, my country," Ho said, suppressing his anger. "Why are you in my country?"

"Cause my country is fighting here," Don answered. "We're at war, so I volunteered."

Ho started showing anger, "I mean, why is America here fighting in my country? We don't want you here!"

"Well, Ho, I'm not thrilled about being here with you, either," Don countered. "I don't like or trust you, him, or any other Vietnamese that I've met."

"Why?" Ho asked indignantly.

"Because of the way your people discriminate against the Montagnards," Bendell said. "And kill 'em off when you can get away with it."

Arrogantly Ho responded, "They are inferior to my people."

"Ho, you couldn't make a boil on a Montagnard's ass."

Very angry, Ho snapped, "Why don't you go home!"

"Why don't you go fuck yourself, Slope," Bendell shot back.

Remembering his adversary, the Viet tried to control his temper. "Many Americans want you home, Trung-uy. What about your movie star, Jane Fonda?"

"What about her?" the lieutenant responded.

"Well, she is a traitor, like many others who—"

With a flash Bendell's Montagnard knife whipped in the commando's right hand, the sharp point just touching Ho's Adam's apple. A Jeh bodyguard's foot came down on the stock of the LLDB sergeant's M16, pinning his fingers to the ground. He let up with his foot as the brat eased his hand back and nursed it. A tiny droplet of blood appeared on Ho's throat.

"Jane Fonda's an American, Ho," Bendell said. "I'll say anything I want about her, but don't you dare say anything bad about her or any American. *Ong hieu,* huh?"

Whispering, Ho answered, *"Da toi hieu, Trung-uy. Xin loi."*

The lieutenant sat back, sheathing his knife. The other two breathed a sigh of relief.

"Ho, you better hope I never make general."

Meekly Ho replied, "Why, Trung-uy?"

"Cause first I'd give the Central Highlands back to the Dega. Then I'd put all the good Viets in a boat in the ocean." Don leaned forward. "Next I'd nuke the lowlands and turn it all into a giant fucking parking lot. Then you know what I'd do?"

Bendell pulled out a cigarillo and lit it slowly, then blew a big puff in Ho's face.

He concluded, "I'd sink the boat."

With veiled anger Ho said, "Trung-uy Bendell, you are very prejudiced."

Grinning, Don replied, "Ong Ho, you are right. You and your people made me that way with your prejudice against the Yards."

He rose, smiling broadly, then said sweetly, "Good night. Pleasant dreams."

Whenever Lieutenant Bendell was out in the boonies, he had a normal SOP, standard operating procedure, thanks to the NCOs at Bragg who had baby-sat him. In his hip pocket he carried a tiny nylon hammock, which was strung with parachute suspension cord. Both ends would be tied very tightly between two trees. He would then string an Army poncho in a sloped-roof shape over the top of the hammock. Next he would pound a forked stick into the ground next to the hammock, within arm's reach. He would hang his ammo harness and CAR-15 on it. Two smaller sticks would be stuck down below, and he would place his boots upside down over them to air them out, keep them dry, and discourage poisonous bugs or snakes from crawling in. Lastly he carried a pair of mosquito-net mittens and a head net, bought at an American sporting-goods store, which would easily fold up and go in his hip pocket.

It was the mosquito netting he quickly discarded as he grabbed everything else at the sounds of the early-morning shooting. Don identified the shots as coming from Joe's part of the perimeter, and he quickly got on his jungle boots and ran that way, CAR-15 and harness in tow.

Arriving at Joe's side of the perimeter, he saw numerous Yards hiding behind trees and in foxholes. Joe, however, cup of coffee in one hand, was using the other to relieve his bladder. Joe nodded. "Good morning," he said, and stepped away from the tree, smiling. He drew his Colt .41 and fired it at the jungle hillside across the narrow valley below the company's perimeter.

As Bendell tried to figure out what Joe was doing, an AK-47 fired back from the opposite hill. Don dived behind a tree and stared at Joe, who stood there grinning.

"Morning," Joe said, and laughed. "Sleep well?"

"Till now, sir," Bendell said, thinking Captain Dietrich had flipped out. "What the fuck's goin' on?"

"I'm just trying to pinpoint a little old NVA rifleman over there," Joe replied, pointing at the opposite ridge.

Joe fired again and the sniper shot back, kicking up dirt at Joe's feet.

"Sir, you're fuckin' crazy," Bendell said.

Ignoring Bendell, Joe picked up the handset of the PRC-25 and said, "Got 'im. This is Lackey Alpha . . . those eight-digit coordinates I gave you are right on. You guys got that hillside already plotted, over?"

"Roger, Alpha," came the voice. "You want a Willy Peter round? Over."

"Negative, he'll hide," Joe responded. "Give me a fire-for-effect and stand by to adjust another concentration. Over."

"Wilco," the voice said. "Rounds on the way. Over."

A few seconds later Don heard the very faint booms of 175-mm howitzers.

Joe stepped out again, smiling, and said, "Watch this."

He fired several more rounds, and the sniper shot back immediately. Seconds later the hillside literally exploded under the artillery concentration. Smiling, Joe raised his cup in a toast to Don.

"I'd say we won that one," Joe said. "Now we can go home and you and Sergeant Crotsley can rebuild that church for the Yards that the VC keep burning down."

Don smiled, turned, and walked away shaking his head, then broke out in laughter.

A large crowd of Montagnards crowded in and out the back door of Dak Pek's team house. Don and Ning stood behind a counter selling them bolts of cloth, beads, dried fish, and so on. Above the door, a sign read: DAK PEK COUNTRY STORE. Joe walked up and looked in, and Don walked out to him, opening a beer.

"Well, how's your company store working out?" Joe asked.

"Well, the Viets don't like it at all, Dai-uy," Bendell replied. "We've knocked out the black market in Dak Pek by selling everything at cost."

Everyone but Don and Joe scattered for cover as rifles, machine guns, and grenades started going off just outside the perimeter.

Commo Willy ran out of the team house and yelled,

"Sir, it's Dak Wen Tung [a nearby village]! NVA are kicking the shit out of them!"

Joe turned and started barking orders at the Americans who poured in from their duty stations.

"Willy, get on the horn and get us a FAC! Bendell, grab that .50!" Pointing, he yelled, "Sergeant Crotsley, start smoking that four-deuce mortar. Move it!"

Joe ran to the .50-caliber closest to the village and started firing at the NVA. In the meantime Bendell ran to the other .50 over his bunker and began firing, and at the same time Larry Crotsley and Larry Vosen popped 4.2-inch mortar rounds into the air.

Somebody shouted, "They're running! They're running!"

Joe Dietrich disappeared below the sandbags around the big gun.

One of the NCOs ran over to Bendell and yelled, "Hey, Lieutenant, Captain Dietrich's been hit! Right in the crotch!"

Running, Don shouted, "Call for a medevac quickly and get the medic!"

Joe Dietrich stood up, holding his bloody groin. He looked around and said, "Someone get the Bac-Si with a bandage. I've got a hole in me someplace."

Laughing, Commo Willy walked up and pointed at the captain's wound and said, "Oh, Captain Dietrich, is your wife gonna be pissed!"

At the hospital, doctors discovered thirty-four separate shrapnel wounds in the captain's legs, testicles, and penis, but the doctors sewed him back together as good as new, except for a few scars, a little inconvenience, and lots of laughs from his men.

Bendell's tiger suit was drenched with sweat as he stood at the base of the mountain east of Ben Het. He knew at the top of the steep trail was his company perimeter and a place to rest. He had called in an air strike on an NVA company, and their mountainous fire-support base was so high up and so steep that he and his men watched from above as Air Force F-4 Phantom jets put in their air strike.

He and Dak Pek's assistant medic were occupying half of the FSB on which Ben Het's XO, Lieutenant Leopold, had been wounded and captured, and their assistant medic, his jaw shot off, had died, leaning against a tree with dead NVA soldiers lying across his legs and at his feet.

The other side of the FSB, across the saddle, was occupied by a Fourth Division 105 battery and a company of infantry. The night before, Bendell's unit had been probed by NVA, and he had walked artillery fire inside his own barbed wire.

The air strike had been to support a patrol of Jeh strikers who had run into NVA. Bendell, Nhual, and ten Jeh strikers, as well as another lieutenant, a Fourth Division platoon leader, and ten GIs had gone down the mountainside on a combined bomb damage assessment patrol.

The patrol was taking a break, the Americans, including Bendell, smoking but sweating profusely and exhausted. The Jeh, however, were laughing and joking with each other while burning leeches off their calves with either cigarettes or Army insect repellent.

Bendell had just removed seven new leeches from his legs and was speaking to the Fourth Division officer. "Fuckin' BDA patrol. Doesn't matter what our report is. Somebody up the line will add a phony body count so it'll look good on the six-o'clock news."

"Speaking of body counts," the other officer said, laughing, "how'd you like calling 105 fire in almost on top of your position last night?"

"Loved it like the clap."

"Officers don't get the clap. Remember," the lieutenant, still chuckling replied, "we get nonspecific urethritis."

One of his soldiers, lying on his back, complained, "Hey, sir, how come we go on a patrol with these fuckin'

ARVNs? They never fight or have to hump. All they do is sit on fire-support bases!''

"Shut up, soldier," the lieutenant said, embarrassed.

"Yes, sir!"

Bendell jumped up and, red-faced with anger, said to the other officer, "I'll take point! Tell your men to keep up!" Yelling at the entire patrol, he said, "Break's over! On your feet! Ba Nua, c'mon, we're taking point."

"Okay, Trung-uy," Nhual said, sensing Bendell's anger.

The angry lieutenant started up the almost vertical mountainside, having to pull himself up on small trees.

The Dega followed like mountain goats, followed by eleven huffing and puffing, grumbling Americans. Sides heaving and pouring sweat, his tiger suit stained white from body salt, Bendell kept climbing, his Yards keeping up easily. The Americans had fallen well back before he had ascended a thousand feet. Angry and bullheaded, he kept on although he felt like he was near death.

After what seemed forever he made it up the mountainside and reached the saddle that separated the mountain's twin tops and the two units. He sent his Jeh strikers back to their foxholes and bunkers, but the bodyguards lingered nearby while others fetched them canteens and food. Nhual returned from the perimeter after twenty-five minutes, handing Bendell some salt pills and fresh water.

"Thanks, Ba Nua," Don said, taking the pills, "It's been half an hour," he said, looking at his scuba watch. "Here they come."

The American patrol, totally exhausted and spent, appeared at the edge of the jungle and struggled the fifty feet up to Bendell. Time for his macho tools, the Green Beret stood tall and lit his Eastwood trademark. One GI was literally being held up by two buddies while two more carried his gear. The lieutenant, looking more like death than life, stopped by Bendell. Don stopped the earlier complainer.

"Soldier, my men are not ARVNs! They have nothing to do with South Vietnamese Army! They are Montagnard warriors and are members of the CIDG or Civilian Irregular Defense Group! In other words, they're mercenaries. They hump three times as many klicks per day as any American unit, and they kick the shit out of the NVA and the VC ten times as often!"

Furious, the commando officer kept on. "Everything they do, or any thing that Special Forces does in 'Nam, your unit and all the other conventional units get the news headlines for it! One Jeh warrior could eat you and ten of your buddies for breakfast and shit you in the jungle! Don't ever compare the Yards with the Vietnamese again! Understand?"

"Yes, sir, I'm sorry, sir," the worn-out Spec Four replied.

The lieutenant then addressed Don. "Lieutenant Bendell, I apologize for my men's comments."

The Green Beret lieutenant thought a second and grinned, waving off the apologies. "Havin' good ol' C rations in an hour, Lieutenant. You're invited for supper."

An hour later Nhual and Bendell prepared C rations over their fire as the Fourth Division platoon leader approached, followed by twenty or thirty American soldiers. The GIs went to various striker's cooking fires and were soon trading boxes of C rations for other items.

"Your Montagnards certainly impressed my men today," the leg lieutenant said. "They really respect them."

"Well, the Yards will definitely love your men," Bendell said with a chuckle. "They brought food."

The assistant medic emerged from a bunker and walked over, nodding to the Dak To lieutenant.

"Sir, I just talked to Dak Pek. Captain Dietrich's gone. He went back to the world," the Bac-Si said. "He's being replaced by a newly activated National Guard captain from Oklahoma. S'pose to be a nice guy."

"Oh, fuckin' beautiful," Bendell said sarcastically. "A

weekend warrior that's never heard a shot fired in anger. What else is going to happen?''

Lying on his cot in his cramped and damp little bunker, Don was becoming delirious. Joe Howard had been gone for a while, and Bendell and Ning had had the entire bunker to themselves. Months before, he had gone to her uncle and given him pigs, chickens, beads, cloth, and rice for her betrothal. According to Jeh tradition, the engaged couple would sleep and live together for one year, with only heavy petting allowed. Then they would marry and make love. He and Ning had broken with tradition as often as possible. He had planned to divorce and stay with the Montagnards, fighting in the war to its victory, then stay on with the Dega and fight their war for autonomy until victory.

He wasn't thinking of these things at this time. Ning sat next to him, tears streaming, as she bathed his face with a cold washcloth.

"Don, don't die," she cried. "Please don't die? I love you too many forever!"

The team medic ran in the door, black bag in hand, pulled out a stethoscope, and started checking Bendell's vital signs.

"What happened, Ning?" he asked.

"He get *beaucoup* hot . . . speak crazy!" she cried. "Been sick, hot, headache bad one month, no tell!"

Feeling Don's forehead, he said, "Go wake up Commo Willy. Tell him I said to get a medevac here quick."

The team CO, Captain Sellers; the medic; Nhual; Ning; and several NCOs watched over a delirious Bendell, lying on a stretcher at the Dak Pek helipad. While the Americans ran out to direct the incoming dust-off helicopter, Ning, crying hard, knelt and kissed him hard and long. He smiled weakly.

She whispered in his ear, "I go find you, they take you

away. Listen, Don, no die. You no give up. I love you one thousand!''

Team members picked him up as the medevac landed, and the NCOs put him in the chopper. Ning ran away into the darkness, crying.

Bac-Si yelled to the dust-off crew chief, ''His temperature is one hundred six point four and rising. I gave him quinine IV. All the A-teams between here and Pleiku will light your way back with parachute flares. Don't hit any mountains!''

The crew chief signaled thumbs-up and the dust-off rose into the sky and turned south, heading toward a distant corridor of flares.

Bendell opened his eyes and looked down. He had an IV needle and tube dripping liquid into each arm. Apparently he was in a hospital ward, but Don didn't know it was in Pleiku. Two giant fans were aimed at him from the base of his bed. For a moment, he thought they were Mohawk aircraft flying at him and then realized what they were. In the previous days, when his temperature had soared over 108 degrees, nurses had ripped off his pajamas, packed ice on his neck, groin, and armpits, and turned on the fans.

Don was not aware of this, as he had been semicomatose for some time.

''Lieutenant Bendell, can you hear me?'' The doctor stared, and Don tried to reason out what was happening, ''Do you know where you are?''

''What's happening?'' Bendell asked.

Smiling, the doctor answered. ''You've been very sick and in a coma.''

''Drowsy,'' Don said. ''Sick? With what? What sick?''

The doctor grinned and answered, ''Falciprium malaria, infectitious hepatitis, amoebic dysentery, methemoglobimeria, anemia, and dengue fever. How did you ever keep yourself alive? I'm sending you to Tokyo and they'll send you home."

Tears welling in his eyes, Don, still not understanding, felt panic nonetheless. "Home! Ning! Nhual! The Montagnards!"

He fainted.

Turning to the nurse, the doctor said, "He's out again. What did he say, nurse?"

Ning showed her papers to the Air Force crew chief and boarded the C7A Caribou aircraft, a small cloth bag in hand. Nhual watched from the American's hilltop as it took off.

He spoke softly to himself. "Good-bye, Ning, you won't find him. Nobody will ever see you again."

He turned as the plane took off and walked slowly into the American team house.

...21...

THE INCREDIBLE JOURNEY

Montagnards and Cambodians scrambled frantically. H'Li, holding their second baby, a daughter, in her arms, fought to keep Kok from putting her on the big cargo plane. Their first son, Thomas, stood next to her.

Crying, she screamed, "You've done enough, Kok. Come with us!"

"No, I cannot go. You go and I will find you later in Phnom Penh. Don't worry, H'Li," Kok said, "I love you, but I must stay and fight. Since Sihanouk was deposed, the North Vietnamese Army is attacking all over Cambodia. We have many FULRO forces in this country. Take care of our children, H'Li."

"Kok! Kok, it is over six hundred kilometers to Phnom Penh, and you are surrounded!" she cried. "What if you can't get through?"

A Cambodian soldier took her gently by the arm and tried to lead her back from the open door. She waved frantically.

"I will make it, H'Li! Don't worry!" Kok yelled.

Crying harder, H'Li yelled, "I love you!"

The door closed and the plane's engines revved up for takeoff. Battle sounds grew closer. Kok waved at the plane and took off running, M16 in his hand.

Kok spent that night in a foxhole with a friend, Y Tieng

Buon Krong. That night, seventy FULRO warriors and thirty Khmer Krom soldiers repelled a large and vicious NVA attack, killing over eight hundred NVA soldiers. For months afterward the NVA executed any man, woman, or child they found from Mondulkiri Province, Cambodia.

The following night again found Kok and Y Tieng fighting against an incredible assault. Before too many hours, they heard tremendous firing and yelling behind them, along with screams of pain and crying. Soon they heard the voices behind them in their perimeter speaking Vietnamese, not Dega or Cambodian. The realization hit them that the NVA had overrun their position. They turned just in time and started firing at the enemy. Laying down a heavy volume of automatic fire from their M16s, Kok and Y Tieng successfully withdrew down the mountain and into the relative safety of the jungle. On top of the hill, they could still hear the cries of men, women, and children being raped, tortured, and killed.

A force of NVA pursued them as they fled all night through the jungle, losing the enemy by morning. Eating fruits, nuts, and berries, they fled for three days and nights before running into Cambodian soldiers walking to Kratie Province to surrender to the NVA.

"Are you Cambodian soldiers?" Kok asked.

"Yes."

"Where you go?"

"Kratie Province," one answered.

"That's northwest," Kok said to Y Tieng. Then he said to the soldiers, "Can you take us there?"

"Not with you carrying rifles," the unarmed soldier answered. "We don't want the communists to kill us."

"You surrender and they will, but we will never surrender," Kok replied. "Just point the way, we will go."

"I will tell you how to find the province chief," the soldier continued. "He has one hundred and fifty men with him, fifty are FULRO, and he goes to Kratie to surrender also. Where do you go?"

"Phnom Penh," Kok replied.

"Phew!" the soldier exclaimed. "You will never make it. It is over six hundred kilometers of enemy. Villagers won't sell you food or they will be killed. You won't make it! It is monsoon season!"

"Then we will die," Kok answered firmly. "But we won't surrender, ever!"

"You are crazy!" the soldier cried.

"And you are cowards," Kok replied emphatically, and stared them down until they turned, unspeaking, and walked away.

Kok and Y Tieng took the trail to Kratie, bypassing the soon-to-be prisoners, and prayed it was the right way. During the monsoon season it was nearly impossible to establish which direction was which.

They walked days and slept under trees at night, carrying nothing but their rifles and the clothing they wore. The next day and night they did the same. Food was more scarce, and they started eating leaves also. Another day and a night passed, and still another.

Nine days after their position was overrun, Kok and Y Tieng still trudged along exhaustedly. All of a sudden large tears began rolling down both men's cheeks. They glanced at each other and broke out sobbing, but they kept on, knowing they were starving to death, literally.

Thirty miles east of Kratie, they ran into the province chief and his one hundred fifty men. They were offered food and fell on it like vultures on a ripe corpse in the desert. Kok chewed and swallowed and closed his eyes in prayers of gratitude.

They remained two more days, argued about what to do, and ate. They argued more, ate more. They made a decision and ate.

The province chief and his one hundred Khmer planned to go to the now occupied Kratie Province and surrender. Ten FULRO members were going back to their homes in

Vietnam. Kok, Y Tieng, and the other forty would go on to Phnom Penh.

The forty started out, but after three days Kok and his comrades were starving again. They had to avoid all villages, as the entire territory was occupied by NVA and they knew frightened villagers would tell on them, anyway.

One of them was Kok's friend, Kpa Doh, who outranked Kok and was leading. Coming upon a water buffalo, one of the warriors shot it. The entire group ran and hid in the jungle.

Kok argued with Kpa Doh about going back for the meat and warned that the shot would have attracted the enemy. Finally Kok said he was leaving and headed for Phnom Penh. The group decided to follow, even Kpa Doh, but he assigned fifteen men to stay behind, butcher the buffalo, and bring the meat.

The next morning at daybreak the group of twenty-five were awakened by the sounds of men on the road below the wooded hillside where they had slept. A company of North Vietnamese were marching their fifteen compatriots down the road single-file, necks bound and linked to the man behind and in front by barbed wire. Their bleeding wrists were also bound with barbed wire. The survivors watched in stunned silence.

Their group kept off the road, hiding at one point when they heard distant gunfire. Before nightfall they came to their now fallen comrades, bodies riddled with bullets, lying alongside the road. They marched on in quiet despair.

The next morning, the twenty-five starving warriors found themselves outside a Cambodian village.

"We are hungry and must go in and buy food," Kpa Doh said. "Move slowly, look for food, but be careful."

"Kpa Doh, listen," Kok pleaded. "It is too quiet. It is a trap. Don't go."

Angry, Kpa Doh said, "You are a coward, Kok?"

Temper and ego flaring, Kok stepped forward in front of the group and marched into the village.

Over his shoulder he said, "Come ahead, then. Watch our people die, but I die with you."

"Me too!" Y Tieng said with finality as he walked up next to Kok.

Kok whispered to Y Tieng, "We are in front. If the NVA ambush us, fire and yell and run straight through the village. They won't expect it."

"Okay."

Sure enough, within two minutes the patrol was blasted by NVA guns from virtually every hut.

"Go!" Kok yelled as he and Y Tieng rushed forward, firing left and right, front and rear, as they ran. He noticed eight FULRO warriors go down in the first fusillade of bullets. He also saw several NVA soldiers rush out of huts and pursue him and Y Tieng as they rushed headlong into the thick jungle growth surrounding the village. Kpa Doh and the other survivors had withdrawn immediately.

Kok and Y Tieng rushed through wet green leaves and branches. It was a many-limbed emerald monster trying to grab and hold them for the shouting, cursing pursuers close behind. A solid green maze, the jungle here was so thick, it was like running the length of a wide, winding hedgerow, right through its middle.

They didn't know where they were heading; they saw only green. They heard only their own gasping breaths torn from their lungs, bullets cracking overhead, and shouted curses behind them in the language of the Yuan.

They burst free of the clutching jade monster. In front of them stood the village from which they had escaped. An NVA spotted them, shouted, and fired. They turned and plunged again into the hot, wet, emerald-green nightmare.

Again they were pursued through thick jungle, and again, disoriented, ran out of it into the village. Once more they were spotted, shot at, and pursued into the morass of vines, leaves, and branches. This time, however, they managed to maintain a beeline from the village and out of the communists' grasp. They were also separated from the other FULRO warriors.

Days later Kok and Y Tieng, clothes tattered and torn, struggled along a heavily used trail. A slight drizzle started, and fog rose from the jungle around them. They felt as if each leg were mired in deep wet cement; each step seemed likely to tear out their hip sockets. Still, they staggered forward.

"Kok, how many more days? I am weak," Y Tieng said. "How many more leaves and roots can we eat?"

Kok started to speak, but both flattened as they heard a laugh behind them. Then they heard Vietnamese voices not twenty feet away. A heavy downpour started as Kok and Y Tieng rolled off the trail, seconds before an unknowing patrol of twenty North Vietnamese soldiers passed over Kok and Y Tieng's tracks. The third NVA, thinking it a rock or root, stepped on the back of Y Tieng's hand. Kok clapped his hand over Y Tieng's mouth as he started to cry out.

The patrol laughed as the two Dega stared after them. Sides heaving, they rolled over onto their backs and laughed at the sky and the vicious rain now pelting their faces and bodies.

Blinking off raindrops, Kok laughed and said, "Y Tieng, it could be worse. We could have no water too."

Y Tieng gave Kok a funny look, and then a belly laugh started down low in both of them, growing into wild guffaws. Tears of laughter spilled down their cheeks as they both rolled into fetal positions, holding their sides during fits of giggling hysteria.

Two days later Kok and Y Tieng stood on the bank of a swollen, wide, rushing river. Covered with cuts and sores, eyes sunken, they looked at the river and then each other.

Resigned, Y Tieng said, "I am not a fish."

Smiling, Kok replied, "But maybe you can be a boat."

"Huh?" Y Tieng said.

An hour later, heads sticking out of the water, Kok and Y Tieng pushed two rafts across the river. Each was made of eight-foot sections of bamboo and held each man's rifle, ammo, and clothing. The two rafts were tied to each other so the raging torrent couldn't separate the two weary warriors.

It had been over three weeks since the journey started. Kok and Y Tieng heard a rooster crow as the sun peeked out above thatched rooftops. They parted the thick foliage at the jungle's edge and looked at the awakening village.

"What do you think, Kok?"

"We are starving, Y Tieng," Kok answered. "We can try to buy food. You stay here and I'll go into the village."

"No, you shoot better," Y Tieng replied. "I'll go and you cover me."

"Okay, but be careful."

Kok's rifle barrel pushed through the leaves as Y Tieng carefully walked into the village. He went forward slowly, gaining confidence with each step. With a start he spun to face three NVA soldiers who ran from the first hut he passed.

Each wore a khaki uniform and a pith helmet with a bright red star on it. Two aimed SKS rifles at Y Tieng, and the third, a menacing leer on his face, an AK-47. Unmoving, Y Tieng slowly raised his hands, trying to swallow his Adam's apple at the same time.

"Time to die, *Moi*," the one with the AK said sadistically.

"*Dung roi!*" came Kok's voice as the three surprised NVA whirled to their left, staring into the barrel of Kok's M16. Above the barrel, they looked into angry eyes.

"*Di au qui-thon*," Kok said menacingly. "*Cong san bac Viet.*"

Swinging his rifle left to right and back again on automatic, Kok actually hit the three Communists with nineteen out of the twenty bullets in his magazine before any of the three, now dead, hit the ground. Nerves spasming, the finger of the dead NVA with the AK-47 tightened on the trigger, spewing thirty bullets into the corpse of his buddy next to him, severing him at the waist. By the time the sporadic, telltale, tinny, metallic sounds of the AK had stopped, Kok and Y Tieng were well on their way through the thick jungle.

The rain had stopped soaking the gaunt-looking pair. It had been two days since their last meal, near the village. Hunger pangs clutched at their insides and quit-demons pulled hard on their legs. Coming to the base of a large tree, the noontime sun beating them into submission, the two collapsed at its base and slept. They slept the sleep of the dead but awakened before dark.

"Kok, I cannot go anymore. I am dead," Y Tieng said. "You go on."

"Don't talk like that, Y Tieng," Kok pleaded. "Get up! Don't quit!"

"I cannot get up," he said weakly. "I am starving to death. My strength is gone."

"You are Dega! Get up, you coward!" Kok screamed. "Get up and walk!"

"You won't make me mad, Kok, but thanks," the other said softly. "Save yourself. Go on."

"You! You stupid Montagnard!" Kok yelled, this time out of real frustration. "Stand up!"

Y Tieng was already unconscious. As if this were a silent signal to quit, Kok started crying and fell on the ground, crying and praying. Within a minute he was fast asleep.

"Kok! The enemy hit me!" Y Tieng's voice screamed as Kok's mind traveled up out of the dark abyss into realization. "Take cover!"

Kok blinked into the early-morning light as he hid behind the tree, M16 in hand. Y Tieng was rubbing his head.

Kok looked up and started laughing as Y Tieng tried to quiet him.

"There's your enemy," Kok said, pointing up into the tree.

Y Tieng looked up to see a monkey among the branches. It was pulling pieces of fruit and throwing it at the two Dega. The branches above were sprawling and bent down from the weight of all the fruit. Y Tieng laughed and cried with joy.

The following day, stomachs full, the pair, wearing their trousers like rucksacks, full of fruit, started out again. They had also tied vines around their waists and filled their shirts with the life-sustaining fruit. They still didn't know what it was, but the monkey ate it, so they did too.

The following day, magnetizing themselves to the sound of far-off "big guns," Kok and Y Tieng walked into a United States mechanized infantry battalion headquarters. They were given more food and supplies at the battalion's higher headquarters in Tay Ninh and were escorted to the Vietnam-Cambodia border. From there they made an easy walk to a unit of Lon Nol troops.

Addressing the Cambodian commander, Kok asked, "Are you Lon Nol troops?"

"Yes, we are," the colonel replied. "Who are you?"

Kok answered, "Sir, I am Ksor Kok, and my friend is Y Tieng. We fought with Colonel Les Kosem. We escaped the communists when we were overrun in Mondulkiri Province."

Shocked, the colonel said, "How did you get here?"

"We walked, sir. We fought, swam, and crawled," Kok said, chest out. "Sir, can you please get us to our families in Phnom Penh?"

Amazed, the colonel offered them both seats and smiled. "Yes, very soon. Yes, we can," he said.

H'Li was dusting a windowsill and humming. She stopped, a shiver running up her spine. Turning slowly, she stared, tears welling up in her eyes and a smile slowly appeared on her face. Standing in front of her was Kok. Khmer National Army uniform on with first lieutenant's rank, he ran forward, arms open. They kissed long and hard, both crying for joy. Kok stepped back and smiled.

... 22 ...

A YUAN VICTORY

Kok walked in the door of his house and tossed his uniform and hat on a table. He heard strange noises from the back of the house, immediately he pulled a pistol from its holster.

Carefully, back to the wall, he inched himself to the door of the hallway. Kneeling, he peeked quickly into the hall and jerked his head back. Seeing nothing, he dived into the hall, gun swinging left and right. The sounds grew louder.

He found H'Li crying in the back bedroom, rubbing their baby daughter's forehead with a damp rag. Kok holstered his gun and ran to her, concerned, knitting his brow. H'Li threw her arms around his neck, sobbing.

"Oh, Kok," she cried, "our little girl is very sick. She has diarrhea bad and is burning up with fever."

Kok grabbed the little girl in his arms and ran for the door.

"Get Thomas and come on," he commanded. "We must get her to the hospital."

Three hours later Kok and H'Li fell asleep on the bench across from their daughter's bed. H'Li stirred and whimpered. Thomas, their son, lay at her side.

"Shhh," Kok whispered. "The doctor said she should be all right. You rest, H'Li. Relax."

H'Li snuggled up closer under his protective arm, a faint smile appearing on her sleeping face.

In the middle of the night Kok awoke with a start. He saw the Vietnamese nurse at the same time she looked up and saw him. She pulled a needle out of his daughter's arm and ran as Kok jumped up. H'Li awakened with a start as Kok started to chase the nurse, then stopped and ran back to his daughter.

He held her in his arms, tears streaking down his cheeks, as the little girl's body convulsed violently. Kok and H'Li stared at each other helplessly . . . and hopelessly. The shaking got more violent as Kok held her tighter and stroked her black hair.

"Oh, God, please save her," he prayed.

Then suddenly the shaking stopped and her little body went limp. He looked down at her face and laid her gently back on the bed. H'Li threw herself into his arms, sobbing heavily.

Kok stared past H'Li at the far wall, tears rolling down his cheeks.

"The Yuan have beaten us," he said sadly, "with the only way they know how to fight."

He looked down at his dead daughter, now at peace, away from war and discrimination. Murdered, nonetheless, by an enemy of his race.

On the other side of the world Don Bendell, now a civilian, a disc jockey, walked in and looked at his baby daughter, Brooke. She slept peacefully in her crib. He smiled and thought of a little girl named Plar. A tear rolled down his cheek. He bent and kissed his daughter.

Leaving Brooke's room, he stopped and looked up, whispering, "Thank you, God. Please protect the other little children."

... 23 ...

DOWN THE ROAD

A master sergeant, green beret on his head, walked past the sign that read: FORT BRAGG BOXING CLUB. He entered the door to find GIs working out, jumping rope, shadow-boxing.

He stopped a young boxer leaving through the door. "Soldier, I'm looking for a civilian named Don Bendell, who's supposed to be teaching karate classes here."

"Back there, Sarge," the boxer replied, and went out the door.

The big red-haired NCO walked to the back of the club and saw Bendell, in karate uniform and long hair, addressing a class full of soldiers in karate garb. Seeing the NCO, Don summoned up a heavyweight brown belt.

"Sergeant Black, take over class for a few minutes, please," Bendell said.

The brown belt bowed. Bendell bowed back and walked over to the sergeant. The two shook and exchanged names.

"Mr. Bendell . . ." the sergeant began.

"Don."

"Don," he said, "I was told you're always lookin' for word on the Yards."

"Yes, I am," Bendell said. "Got anything?"

"Just a rumor," the sergeant replied. "But I heard you'd be interested. Heard a Cambodian officer is attending a course at Fort Eustis and he's gone to the government asking for political asylum. Wants to get his family out of Phnom Penh 'fore it falls.''

"Yeah?" Don said.

"Reason I thought you'd like to know is that talk is he ain't really a Cambode.'' The NCO smiled. "He's a Jarai and is chief of staff of FULRO.''

Bendell smiled. "Well, thanks, that's good to know. I hope his family makes it.''

Don didn't know at the time that it was Kok Ksor, as he would be called in America.

...24...

OUT OF THE TIGER'S MOUTH

The twin-engine plane sat helplessly on the tarmac at the Phnom Penh airport as Khmer Rouge rockets and mortars erupted around it. The cacophony of sounds from the explosions, combined with the screams from would-be passengers, added to H'Li's hysteria as she tried hard to fight back the panic that now gripped her. Her baby son, Jonathan, in her womb, and her other three sons—Thomas, John, and Daniel—in tow, she ran back and forth in the frightened crowd, waving frantically at her American friend, Dr. Mooneyham, a missionary who was looking out the plane's window.

Tears welled up in the mother's eyes as she saw the plane's door close. The realization hit her at the same time that Dr. Mooneyham couldn't possibly see her amid all the other screaming, waving Asians.

Phnom Penh had been under siege and was falling to the brutal Peking-backed Khmer Rouge. She had already been told that Y Bham Enoul; his vice president, Kpa Koi; and other FULRO leaders had sought refuge at the French embassy. She had heard all the horror stories about the Khmer Rouge, and she knew that Y Bham and Kpa Kok would not be safe.

Her husband, Kok, was safe in America now and had applied for political asylum to get her and her sons out of

Cambodia. He was now chief of staff of the FULRO, and she knew that was an automatic death sentence for her and her four young sons if caught.

Kok, now undercover as an officer in the Khmer (Cambodia) National Army, had been flown to the U.S.A. to take the Transportation Officers Basic Course at Fort Eustis, Virginia. He had come back to her and later had returned to America to take the Transportation Officers Advanced Course. He had just completed it and, unbeknownst to H'Li, had been watching network TV news one night in Virginia when he saw pictures of his sons' grade school, demolished by Khmer Rouge rockets. He had gone to every American official, missionary, and citizen that he knew. He had begged, pleaded, and tried everything he could think of to get help to bring his family to America. Several Americans did care. Money was provided and red tape cut.

Unfortunately H'Li's passport and papers were in the hands of a Mr. So, who was nowhere in sight. He was supposed to have delivered them earlier. She knew that Dr. Mooneyham could help her, but he couldn't see her. She felt like a person who had been tied to an anchor and dropped in a lake with her face just two inches from the surface. She could see sunshine and fresh air but couldn't breathe it into her bursting lungs.

H'Li heard one of the plane's engines start up, and she started sobbing. She had faced death many times in her life but never had known true freedom. She wanted this for her sons more than anything. She and Kok were two of just a handful of Dega with any schooling, let alone a high-school education. Kok was going to attend college in America. Her people needed that desperately.

The crowd screamed as a rocket landed nearby. Everyone dived to the ground. H'Li huddled over, protecting her unborn son, as her oldest little boy, Thomas, lay down, covering his two brothers, John and Daniel, with his torso and arms.

She heard the plane's second engine sputter and stood up. It wouldn't start.

Tears streaming, H'Li looked skyward with crying people lying all around her feet. A big grin spread across her face.

"Thank you, Heavenly Father," she said.

"H'Li! H'Li!" a voice cried.

She turned to see Mr. So running toward her, waving the passports. She turned and looked at the plane. The door had opened, and the copilot ran down and started checking the bad engine. People started standing again, as Mr. So fought his way through the crowd. He handed H'Li the papers, and tears in her eyes, she tried to speak.

"I know! I know!" He smiled and yelled above the noise. "Go on!"

Grabbing her sons, H'Li broke through the crowd and ran to the gate. A guard went through her papers and took her tickets. She looked at the copilot, shrugging his shoulders and shaking his head at the pilot, as if he didn't know what the engine problem was. The pilot signaled him to load up. She felt the panic again as the guard carefully perused her passport. She was cleared to go.

The steps started to go up on the plane as she burst through the gate, her sons being dragged behind her. H'Li fought to keep her bladder from letting go. Reaching the plane just as the door closed, her heart skipped a beat, but she breathed a sigh of relief as it reopened. The smiling copilot lowered the steps and they boarded. The door closed as H'Li fell into a seat, and she saw the second engine start up with no trouble.

Within minutes H'Li and her four sons were flying toward Kok . . . and freedom.

... 25 ...

THE WAR WITHIN

Don Bendell lay on his back moaning, writhing, and twist-
ing his head from side to side. Whimpers escaped his lips
as the pleasure of Ning's loving built in his loins.

As his love poured forth, Ning continued to draw it
from him, until she filled herself with all of his energy,
leaving Bendell totally spent and exhausted.

He lay panting, experiencing new sensations as she
started kissing her way back up his body. He looked at
her face and smiled. It was Shirley, his wife, and not Ning.
Wait, he thought, How could that be? He smiled and
thought how much he loved Shirley.

With a crash his bunker door flew open and NVA soldiers, armed with AK-47s, crowded into the tiny, rat-
infested underground bunker. In a millisecond Bendell
threw his body over Shirley's, grabbed his .357 Magnum
in one hand, his CAR-15 in the other. Cocking the pistol
and flipping the little rifle's selector on to auto with his
thumb, he fired quickly, efficiently, and expertly.

In less than two seconds all three NVA lay on the damp
floor, their blood draining into the dirt. Guns still in each
hand, Don wrapped his arms around the wide-eyed Dega
beauty and they both sighed with relief. All of a sudden
an object flew in through the door and hit the bunker floor,

rolling to a stop at Don's footlocker. It was a Chicom (Chinese communist) hand grenade.

"Grenade!" Don screamed as he sat up, heart pounding and sweat pouring.

Eyes open now, he looked around. He was in a water bed, a fireplace and a bookcase beyond his feet. Shirley woke and sat up, grabbing his shoulder.

"What's wrong, honey?" she asked, concern on her face.

"Nightmare, Shirl. It's all right."

"Vietnam again?" she asked.

"Yeah, and it's been way over ten years," Don replied with frustration. "I don't know why this has started up."

He thought back to a day in 1975. He owned a karate school outside Fayetteville and taught at Bragg. He and his first wife were in a hamburger joint when a pregnant woman walked in with a Green Beret sergeant first-class in dress greens. It was Commo Willy.

Don had learned that Dak Pek had been overrun by the NVA Second Division. All the Americans, Nhual, his family, and others had been blown up by satchel charges with simultaneous timing devices. Only Commo Willy and the team sergeant, Sergeant Weeks, who had been there as heavy weapons sergeant when Bendell first arrived, had survived. The two had fought bravely, both earning Silver Stars, and had been extracted by helicopter along with Don's pet dog, Ambush, just minutes before Dak Pek and the swarming NVA were flattened by a B-52 strike. Half of the LLDB team had turned out to be communist agents.

"I love you," Shirley said, gently kissing Don's shoulder.

Choking up, Don said, "I love you too. So much."

He started crying, racking sobs, as he and Shirley threw their arms around each other. He cried as she stroked his hair lovingly.

• • •

Five hundred miles away, H'Li again said, "Kok! Kok!"

Hearing the shower still running, she walked over to the bathroom door and yelled, "Kok! Kok!"

Still hearing no answer, H'Li flung the door open and let out a cry as she saw Kok lying unconscious half in and half out of the shower. She ran to him crying, picked him up, and held him in her arms.

"Thomas!" she yelled. "Dial 911! Call ambulance!"

Moonlight rippled across the dew-covered grass. It ran up and surrounded the base of the large oak tree. The first thick limb forked out at a height of eight feet. Two bare feet could be seen unmoving at the base of the thick branch. They ran up to two squatting legs, capped with a pair of white briefs. The slender man's torso was covered with goose bumps from the cool nighttime breeze. In his right hand a gun rested comfortably. A stainless-steel Ruger Super Blackhawk .44 Magnum with a very long barrel, the revolver was loaded with hollow-point bullets. The night breeze stirred Bendell's brown hair, but that's all that moved, except for his hazel eyes, and they homed in on a noise and relaxed as his mind registered it as safe.

"Don, what are you doing?" Shirley asked. "It's two-thirty A.M."

Smiling warmly, Don said, "I heard a noise, honey. Just wanted to make sure my family's safe."

"Don, can you come inside and have a cup of tea," Shirley responded gently. "We need to have a talk."

In another state, the white-haired doctor removed the stethoscope from his ears and smiled warmly at H'Li, who was wringing her hands.

"The answer is simple, Mrs. Ksor. Kok is suffering from exhaustion and needs plenty of rest," the doctor said. "He'll be okay."

"No understand," H'Li said. "Why?"

The doctor started chuckling and replied, "Well, he just got promoted again at work and always works long hours. He is going to college full-time and must study hard for his straight A's. You have four growing sons and live in a strange country. And he spends all the rest of his time writing letters to government officials and VIPs on behalf of his people. Now, Mrs. Ksor," he said, smiling, "why do you suppose he's worn out?"

Don and Shirley were seated at their kitchen table, he drinking tea and she coffee. Shirley had tears in her eyes.

"Yes, it's worrying me. Take tonight, for example," Shirley said quietly. "Honey, you are an ex–Green Beret. You've taught karate and competed for years. Do you think it's normal for you to sit in a tree at two-thirty in the morning, holding a gun and looking for an enemy that never shows up? Vietnam was two wives and many years ago. Why don't you talk to somebody about it?"

"Well, if they could stop the nightmares," Don said with a smile, "it would sure help. Don't you agree?"

"Of course. Listen, pal, you and I have both beaten alcoholism. And for a long time now. Anything else will be a cinch."

Don reached across the table, grabbed her hand, and kissed it lovingly. "You're not only my best friend, I love you very much."

. . . 26 . . .

THE WAR GOES ON

People kept walking in and out of the restaurant. Bendell, now around forty, walked in the door with an executive in a gray business suit. They walked to the restaurant door, but it was very crowded, and a band played loudly in the adjoining bar. The two men walked over to two overstuffed lobby chairs in a relatively quiet corner.

Bendell, still slim and in good shape, wore a burgundy Western leather sport coat, a gray Western shirt, slacks, and gray sharkskin cowboy boots. A gray dress cowboy hat was now in his hand as the two sat down. Next to them was the open door of a darkened office.

"So how was your flight from Washington?" Bendell asked politely.

"Fine, fine, I really enjoy coming to Colorado. So you tell me," the man said, "how's FULRO?"

Don laughed. "Frustrated. Can't you let Kok and me meet with President Reagan or George Schultz?"

The executive looked at Don seriously. "Quite honestly, the State Department wants to know if you are advising FULRO to go back into Vietnam, guns blazing."

A pair of eyes looked at the two from the darkened office. A pair of ears listened to the conversation.

"Look," Bendell replied, "I'm never going to advise anybody to commit suicide. Besides, Kok is president of

FULRO. He makes the decisions; I'm just his senior adviser." Don paused. "I just want to know why nobody from the government with any horsepower will meet with Kok."

"There are a lot of us in the State Department who worked with the Yards in Vietnam, and we all really feel for them," the State Department executive went on, "but officially, quite frankly, the Yards just aren't large enough pawns in the scheme of things worldwide."

Bendell responded angrily, "Pawns! This ain't a fuckin' game, man! The CIA, in 1958 through 1961, promised FULRO over and over that we would take care of the Yards if they would fight for us and the South Vietnamese."

The eyes continued to watch. The ears continued to hear. The eyes were Oriental, dark, and shaded by black eyebrows.

Still angry, Don continued. "Doesn't our word as a government mean anything anymore? The Dega were totally loyal to us during the war. Kok wants to see his people have a democracy identical to the U.S. He doesn't want money, power, or fame. He just wants his people to have the freedom to govern themselves, and to stop the elimination of his race."

The executive put his hands up. "I know, I know, but be realistic, Don. How many Yards are there in the world?"

"Less than nine hundred thousand now," Bendell said. "That's just the point. When I was in 'Nam twenty years ago, there were over three million. Two million didn't die in the war. They have been killed by the Vietnamese, and they won't stop until the Dega are wiped off the face of the earth."

"Why?" the Washingtonian queried.

"Why is there apartheid?" Don countered. "Because some races of people are filled with fear and paranoia and act like total assholes!"

The conversation continued for another half hour while the unseen watcher continued to eavesdrop on the pair.

"How did Kok become president of FULRO?" asked the G-man.

"Well, you already know from CIA files that he was chief of staff, which was third in command," Don answered.

"Yes, I read the file on Kok before I left Washington," he said.

Bendell went on. "In 1976, the Khmer Rouge took Y Bham Enuol and his vice president, Kpa Koi, out of the French embassy in Phnom Penh and executed them both. Kok automatically ascended into the presidency. Now Hanoi wants him dead."

"Why?" the man asked.

"Because he's a threat," Don said. "How do you think the guys in power in Hanoi got there? Just like the little resistance movements that spring up here all the time in the Vietnamese community. You know, ten guys meet together in a basement and start a new VN resistance organization. That's why Hanoi's paranoid. Our agents in France learned from French Intelligence that Hanoi infiltrated 'sappers' into the U.S. through Refugee Site Two in Thailand. They're supposed to target and assassinate resistance-force leaders in the U.S., especially FULRO. Hanoi's very afraid of FULRO. I mean, stop and think," Don kept on, "after Saigon fell in 1975, we had one thousand eight hundred FULRO fighters who kept Ban Me Thuot under siege for five years. You know how?"

The executive shook his head negatively.

Don went on, "The PAVN (People's Army of Vietnam) had all their fancy Soviet and Chicom weapons, tanks, and vehicles. Our fighters broke up in groups of six and hid in the tops of banana trees all day long. At night they'd sneak down and make raids and ambushes. Hanoi's told our representatives in meetings that FULRO is just an annoying mosquito, but quite frankly, they fear FULRO a lot more than that.

"The PAVN are totally paranoid. They have infiltrated agents into the U.S. posing as refugees. An FBI agent told me off the record that they know of at least four political assassinations in Vietnamese neighborhoods."

"Oh, come on, Don," the man said.

He stopped talking as a gray-haired waitress walked across the lobby and into the darkened office, turning on the light. Bendell and the government rep listened as they heard two muffled voices in the office. In less than a minute the older waitress emerged, accompanied by another waitress, her long black hair in a bun and held by a hairnet. She glanced nervously at the two dumbfounded men as she walked by.

The executive looked at Don and said, "She's Vietnamese."

Grinning, Bendell stood up and said, "I rest my case. I took some counseling for a mild case of PTSD and decided the best thing I could do is continue to help the Dega. That was my mission in 1968, and I won't give it up. Just because the government chose to surrender, I decided that I didn't have to. I've got to go. Thanks a lot for flying here and meeting with me. Give my regards to Ronnie."

The two shook hands and Don walked out the door.

... 27 ...

A NEW BEGINNING

Don and Kok rode horses through a beautiful setting of trees, rocks, and pasture in southern Colorado's mountains. In the background rose the majestic, snow-capped Sangre de Cristo Mountains.

No longer in loincloths or tiger suits, Kok wore a pair of faded Levi's jeans, a Ban-lon shirt, and hiking boots. Don wore chaps, spurs, and faded cowboy garb and cowboy hat. Mounted on his powerful black-and-white Appaloosa, Hawk, he looked down at Kok on a wiry little bay mustang.

A red-tailed hawk circled overhead, swirling around and around in a graceful, lazy search for a meal. Two mule deer bounded across the meadow in front of the riders.

"This is beautiful country, brother," Kok said.

Don smiled and looked around. "God's country, Kok. Bet it's a little cooler than the mountains you grew up in."

"You bet." Kok laughed. He got a faraway look in his eye, and then a tear.

Don didn't look over; he knew something was wrong. "What's wrong . . . homesick?" Don asked.

The two stopped and Don tightened the cinches on both horses.

"Yes," Kok said. "It is hot and humid and has tigers

and malaria and monsoons, but it is my home and they took it from our people.''

Don thought a minute and then pointed to a far-off mountain range. ''Four years ago we were riding over in that range and I ran into a grizzly bear. I got out of there fast and didn't tell anybody but the game warden. He's a friend. Know why?''

''No, I don't,'' Kok replied. ''Why?''

Don mounted up, as did Kok, and he continued. ''A few years ago a guy named Ed Wiseman got mauled by a grizzly and killed it down in the San Juans. Everybody said that it was the last grizzly in Colorado. People are afraid of the grizzly, probably because it's so ferocious if you get too close. I didn't want anybody to know, so they wouldn't flood the area looking for it. We invaded the grizzly's country; years ago they were tough and mean and scared us, so we killed them all off.''

''Like the Yuan do to my people,'' Kok said, tears beginning to flow down his cheeks as he continued. ''The grizzly bear is now an endangered species, isn't it?''

''Sure is,'' Don answered.

''You know, I like to watch PBS, and I like to see the *National Geographic Explorer* series. I see how much money and energy Americans spend to save or transplant endangered species of animals. I see how much Americans care about them and try to protect them, but my people are human beings, Brother. They are not animals and they are becoming extinct at the hands of the Vietnamese. Why does nobody care? When my people fought so bravely with the Special Forces and have always been so loyal to America, why are we ignored in Washington? We provide them with some of their best intelligence about American MIAs, and they ignore us. Why? I don't understand?''

Don rode on in silence and stared at the Sangre de Cristos.

Finally he answered, ''My brother, Americans would

care if they knew about it. Look how they fight against apartheid. Washington won't ignore us if the people tell them not to. Without the voice of the people, Washington is just a city with some good caring people, along with a bunch of assholes. Kok, I think it's time that you and I sit down and tell our stories.''

Bendell stopped his horse and so did Kok.

"Kok, you have to understand something," Don added. "if we do this thing, it will expose us and our families to more danger. You have not been able even to write letters to relatives in Vietnam or they will be identified, tortured, and murdered. And you know that I had two Vietnamese drive slowly around my office three times this summer in a silver Mercedes.''

Kok smiled and replied, "I know, my brother.''

Don returned the smile. "I just want you to be sure. Once we do this, Hanoi will really want our heads on a platter.''

Again Kok smiled gently and responded, "You know, getting people to help or even listen to us has been like climbing a tree to catch a fish, but, Don, something has got to be done for my people now!'' He got teary and more emotional as he continued. "Right now, every day in Vietnam, the PAVN come into Dega villages and accuse the best men of being members of FULRO. They take them and drill holes in the backs of their hands and run a wire through the holes and then drag them around the center of the village until they cannot take any more and finally confess that they are FULRO.'' Very emotional now, he kept on. "Then they stand them up and execute them in front of their wives and children. It is horrible, and I can do nothing.''

Still distraught, Kok paused briefly to collect himself. "Don, you and I already know that they are moving Dega all over Vietnam and working them in rice fields and rubber plantations in work gangs. The older ones die every day, all the time. The girls all leave and join our forces to fight because they only give enough food for the mother and father. If the boy is too smart or strong, they kill him.''

Kok was sobbing as Don replied, ''Kok, my brother, George Bush said in his inaugural address that our country keeps its word. We will find out if that was just talk or sincere.''

''But how can we reach his ears, Don?'' Kok added with frustration. ''The CIA employs a Dega who claims to have been a FULRO general, but they don't even look at his age and figure that he had to have been only twelve years old when he supposedly was made general. He tells American families with MIAs that he can locate their loved ones and has information about him, then he steals their savings from them.''

Don laughed and said, ''Kok, half of the idiots that you and I know claim to work for the CIA.''

''Everybody in North Carolina is sure that he works for them. Everybody wants to be a leader. Everybody wants to be in the spotlight. How will Washington know how to . . . uh . . . sort them out?''

Don answered, ''Kok, you and I both have a few friends in the CIA. We have also made friends in other government agencies. They have a big file on you and they keep an eye on us to insure we don't ever deal with communists. Believe me, but you also have to remember what that one guy from the National Security Council said. Remember he told us that whenever anybody mentions FULRO around Washington, people picture a bunch of savages in loincloths running around shooting crossbows at NVA tanks. They don't picture a proud, spiritual, noble race of people who are being slaughtered every single day.''

Tears in his eyes still, Kok replied, ''But when will they help? Our agents in Vietnam and Cambodia tell us that they think our race will be totally extinct in ten years. You mentioned the savages with crossbows; why can't those idiots realize that America pulled out of Vietnam, and our 'savages,' just eighteen hundred of them, cut off all the lines of communications into Ban Me Thuot and held it under siege for five years until we simply ran out of bullets.'' Sarcastically he added, ''Maybe it's because the Dega are so stupid and primitive. We must get help—today . . . not tomorrow.''

''Remember when Don Scott and Jim Morris and the others got the two hundred and nineteen Dega out of Thailand and brought them here? Remember the happiness? That was just the beginning, my brother.''

Don continued. ''One of the greatest things about our country, Kok, is that if the people know, then they will care and will order Washington to give a damn. You and I will be criticized and we'll both be even bigger bull's-eyes for Hanoi, but if the American people find out what has happened and is still happening to your people, they will stop it.''

''How?'' Kok asked.

''First of all, the PAVN make up all kinds of clever plans to go into Dega villages and kill the smartest and strongest, right?'' Don said.

''Right,'' Kok said, smiling.

''Well, Hanoi doesn't even shit without Moscow's permission, and Moscow wants us to be pals. We can also get other governments to help get more Dega refugees relocated. We can get missionary groups working on this,'' Don said, his enthusiasm building. ''Believe me, if we tell the people, the people will handle it.''

Kok smiled broadly. ''I think you are right.''

Don turned his horse. ''We better head back; the Denver Bronco game starts in an hour and H'Li and Shirley said they'd scalp us if we're late.''

''Okay,'' Kok said, turning the mustang.

The two friends rode for a minute, then Kok stopped and Don followed suit.

Kok looked at Don with a giant grin on his face and said, ''You are right. These two old warriors lay dow their crossbows and rifles and pick up their pens and word processors. Dega means 'Sons of the Mountains,' and it is very important for my grandchildren to understand what that means. My brother, the war is not over. We have just begun to fight!''

THE BEST IN WAR BOOKS